Welcome to Mo...
and daring women, where more than fifty tales
of passion, adventure and intrigue unfold
beneath the Big Sky. Don't miss a single one!

Montana
★ MAVERICKS

LISA JACKSON
Lone Stallion's Lady

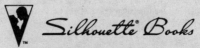

Silhouette Books
Published by Silhouette Books
America's Publisher of Contemporary Romance

Special thanks and acknowledgment to Lisa Jackson
for her contribution to the Montana Mavericks series.

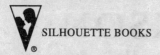 SILHOUETTE BOOKS

ISBN-13: 978-0-373-31043-2

LONE STALLION'S LADY

Recycling programs
for this product may
not exist in your area.

LISA JACKSON

lives with her family in the Pacific Northwest. She has been writing for over twenty years. Her books have appeared on the *New York Times, Publishers Weekly* and *USA TODAY* bestseller lists. Her free time is spent with friends and family.

Prologue

Kincaid Ranch
Whitehorn, Montana

"Well, Laura, I've got some bad news," Garrett Kincaid said as he poured himself a cup of coffee from the enamel pot resting on the remains of the campfire. Dark embers glowed red and the wide night sky twinkled with thousands of stars above this ridge of the Crazy Mountains. Somewhere, not too far away, a coyote howled.

Of course Laura didn't answer. She'd passed away years ago, but after nearly half a century of living with and loving her, he sometimes had to talk to his wife. He believed that a part of her still lingered nearby, if only in his heart.

Squatting near the fire, sipping the hot, bitter brew, he tamped down the loneliness that never quite left him and glanced at his painted stallion, Ricco, who was grazing just beyond the glow of the campfire.

"Now, Laura, even though Larry was our firstborn, you and I both know that he had more than his share of faults." Garrett squeezed his eyes shut. "Larry never thought the rules applied to him. He drank, gambled, smoked and womanized his way into an early grave." A lump filled Garrett's throat and he wondered, not for the first time, if somehow he'd failed his only boy, if he'd been too arrow-straight and unbending for his wayward son. But it was too late for regrets. "Darlin', now that he's gone, too, I hate to bad-mouth him. Hell, I loved him almost as much as you did. I just hope he knew it."

Frowning, Garrett stretched out one leg on the long grass and heard the rush of water from the creek, swollen with the spring runoff that cut through these hills. "Anyway, I've been goin' through his things. I found a strongbox where he kept a lot of personal papers and such. It seems our son didn't quit sowing his wild oats when he was a teenager. Not only that, but he fathered himself a passel of boys. Six. Well, maybe even seven, but I'm not sure about that. I've got a private investigator looking into it."

He paused and watched the moon begin to rise in the broad expanse of sky. Yes, this sure was God's country.

"The investigator's name is Gina Henderson. She's a cute thing, and smart as a whip. Right off the bat she found six of our illegitimate grandsons, Laura. Helluva nice girl, she is. You'd like her." Garrett's lips curved into a smile at the thought of the feisty redhead. "She's gonna come here next week and try to locate Larry's youngest, if the boy really does exist. Anyway, in the meantime I've got to call all our grandsons and tell them about their father, even though they don't have a clue they have Kincaid blood running through their veins." He sighed as a night breeze crept through the hills, rustling the branches of the lodgepole pines at the edge of the meadow.

"Yes, Laura, it's a mess. I sure wish you were here to help me out. I just want you to know that I'm going to make it right, straighten things out with Larry's sons. It darn near breaks my heart to think that our boy was so…well, damned irresponsible—but then, we always knew it, didn't we? Right from the get-go, Larry was a wild one."

Garrett envisioned his wife's pretty face and thought maybe it was better that she hadn't known about all of Larry's indiscretions, hadn't experienced the heartache of realizing there were so many children abandoned by their father. Garrett rubbed his neck and suddenly felt all of his seventy-two years. He drained his cup and tossed the dregs into the fire, causing the coals to sizzle and smoke.

"I'm going to start by calling Trent Remmington. He's not the firstborn by a long shot, but he seems to be the one who most needed a decent father figure in his life. I'm afraid he might be a lot like Larry. Trent's a rebel, struck it big in the oil business and doing okay now, but as a kid, he barely finished high school and gave his mother fits. He and his twin brother, Blake, were passed off as another man's kids and raised by governesses and the like." Garrett snorted at the thought and emptied the coffeepot onto the grass. "Blake, he towed the line. Trent was hell on wheels. A real maverick. Still is, I think." Straightening, Garrett's knees popped and he felt the flare of arthritis in his hip. He kicked dust into the campfire and packed the remains of a sandwich and his coffeepot into his saddlebag. How did you go about telling a man that everything he'd held true in his life had been a lie?

Well, you just did it. Garrett packed up his few belongings and stuffed them into the saddlebag, too. The fire died and he glanced down the hill to the heart of the ranch where a half dozen lights glowed in bright warm patches from the bunkhouse and stables. The silvery illumination of three security lamps reflected onto the roofs of the sheds and the front of the main house. It was empty now. Had been for years.

Well, that was going to change.

God, he missed Laura. She'd been rock-steady throughout all the good and bad times in their marriage. He'd never wanted to outlive her, but a man didn't choose his way into the world, or out of it, either.

Deciding to call Trent in Houston this very night, he ignored the ache in his hip, walked over to Ricco and patted the white splash on the stallion's neck. "Let's go," he said, slinging the saddlebag over the saddle horn, grabbing the reins and swinging himself up.

He heard the coyote's lonesome cry one more time and looked to the sky. A shooting star sizzled across the heavens. Garrett smiled, imagining it a sign from his wife.

"Thanks for listening, darlin'," he whispered into the wind. Pulling on the reins, he and the big stallion headed downhill.

One

"Just slow down a minute, would you?" Trent Remmington half yelled into the crackling cell phone at his ear. Rain pounded the windshield and the crack of thunder was louder than the roar of traffic in this part of Houston. "Who are you? What do you want?" He thought the old man had said something about being his grandfather, but that was impossible.

He maneuvered his BMW through the streets, which were beginning to flood with the sudden torrent. Water sprayed from beneath his tires, the windshield wipers slapped, and some old Garth Brooks's tune pulsed through the speakers. Headlights flashed in his eyes as he turned quickly onto the street where he lived in a high-rise apartment building that he owned outright.

"—Kincaid…my son…your father…dead now and I just found his papers…."

Hell, he couldn't hear a word. "Hang on," he growled, snapping off the radio as the apartment building came into sight. He pressed the automatic parking gate opener, drove into the underground lot and pulled into his private space. The phone went dead.

"Great. Just great." He snapped the phone shut, stuffed it into the pocket of his suede jacket and got out of the car. The shoulders and collar of his jacket were wet, the result of his mad dash from an attorney's office to the car, and the underground garage with its hissing pipes and cement floor was hot and muggy.

Listening for the damned phone to ring, he walked to the elevator, used his key and took a quick ride to the top floor where his suite of rooms—the place he called home in the city—opened up to him. The blinds were up and beyond his leather couches, tables of rosewood, glass and brass was a panoramic view of the city. The windows were steamed, the air-conditioning running full-blast, and through the partially clear glass he could see lightning fork down from the heavens and flash in a brilliance that vied with the glow of Houston's city lights.

He shucked his wet jacket and poured himself a quick drink, wondering if he should sign on the dotted line to sell off half the wells he owned in Wyoming and net more than ten million before taxes. At one time he would have felt a deep satisfaction with the deal, that he'd proved wrong all the nay-sayers who'd thought him a complete failure. Now he didn't really give a damn.

As the Scotch—which cost more per bottle than he'd made in a day's wages when he'd first started out—slid down his throat, he leaned a shoulder against the window-pane and wondered who had called him. Probably some prank or wrong number. The connection had been lousy.

He felt unsettled. Or maybe it was his bad mood. Lately his entire life had turned a corner and he wasn't certain he liked the new direction it was taking. At thirty-two he was restless and edgy, just as he had always been, but he no longer felt the rush from meeting the challenges in his life.

Turning from the window, he tossed back his drink. This change of attitude had all started a few weeks back in Dallas, at an oilmen's convention. It had been boring as hell, until he'd met the redhead. Celia O'Hara. He'd spied her in the patio bar of the DeMarco Hotel and he'd been fascinated. She was sexy, a bit shy, with legs that wouldn't quit and wide green eyes that shifted from sly to naive in a heartbeat. From the minute she'd entered the bar, he'd been hooked. Arrogantly he'd assumed she, like so many other women, would fall for his charms.

But the whole night had blown up in his face.

He wondered what had happened to her—she'd disappeared from his bed in the morning—had even gone so far as to make inquiries.

He should have forgotten her, but he hadn't. He'd even contacted a private investigator. He wasn't used to taking no for an answer, especially when she'd said yes the night before.

The cell phone rang, shattering his thoughts. He pulled it out of his jacket pocket and flipped it open. "Remmington."

"Trent?"

"Yep."

"I called a few minutes ago." Trent recognized the deep voice with the slight Western drawl. He sat on the edge of the sofa. "Don't know how much you heard earlier, so I'll start over."

"That would be a good idea."

"My name's Garrett Kincaid and I'm your grandfather."

Trent sat stock-still, holding the phone to his ear with one hand, the ice in his glass melting in the other.

"I know you think Harold Remmington is your dad and, hell, he should get all the credit, raising you and your brother as he did, but the truth of the matter is that your mother was involved with my son Larry. You two boys were the result."

The man went on and on, and though Trent wanted to call him a raving lunatic and slam the phone shut, there was enough truth peppered into the guy's story that he didn't. Maybe Kincaid was a nutcase, but if so, he was a thoughtful, slow-speaking one, and Trent could detect a note of regret in his voice; honest, down-to-earth remorse.

"...there are others, as well. I want all of you to meet."

"'Others'? I don't get it." The guy was talking about Blake, his twin, of course. Or were there more?

"You will."

"Maybe I don't want to. You know, this is way beyond bizarre, Kincaid."

"You're not telling me anything I don't know. Look, I'm hoping you can arrange your schedule so that you could fly up here to Montana in a week and we can sit down and talk. All of us."

Trent's head was pounding, his ears ringing, and flashes of his childhood whipped across his mind's eye. He and Blake learning to ride bikes, being taught by a baby-sitter. Their mother, Barbara, hadn't been around much. A state commissioner when they'd lived in Montana, she'd been a real go-getter who'd had little if any time for rambunctious twin boys. Boarding schools and governesses had been Barbara's means of parenting. Trent had spent most of his time getting into trouble, calling attention to himself. His twin, however, had tried like hell to be perfect, hoping his mother and father would notice. They hadn't. Barbara had been wrapped up in her career; Harold Remmington had never really given a damn.

"…so much we need to talk about," the caller went on. "I've got plans for you boys—"

"I'm used to making my own plans."

"I know. That's not what I meant." The geezer continued, "But since we're a family now, I'd like to meet all of you."

"'Family'?" Trent sneered. "You think you're part of my family?"

"Yes, son, I do."

"Give up the Aw-shucks-cowboy routine, would you? I mean, this is one helluva lot to digest, and I don't even know if you're legit or a first-class nutcase or someone intent on shaking me down. An hour ago my life was just the way it's been for thirty-two years, and now you expect me to buy that everything I believed in is wrong."

"That's about the size of it."

"Damn."

"Come on up to Whitehorn. Meet the rest of the family out at the ranch. It's the only way you'll know for sure if I'm the real deal or—what did you call me?— 'a first-class nutcase.'" The old man's voice sounded a bit crafty for the first time. His gravelled chuckle seemed like pebbles rattling inside a wooden box. "Well, maybe I am. Anyway, you may as well come to the ranch. What have you got to lose?"

"Well, that's a good question, isn't it?"

Kincaid ignored the sarcasm, gave him directions to the ranch and hung up.

Trent swallowed the remains of his watery drink and walked directly to the bedroom closet. No way would he wait a week. He pulled out a battered leather bag and flung it onto the bed. Ignoring the suits and sports jackets hanging near the power ties in his closet, he went to the bureau, found a couple pairs of scruffy jeans and some shirts that did the jeans justice and tossed them onto the bed. He only paused long enough to leave a few long-winded voice mails for his secretary and his foremen, giving last-minute instructions and telling them to reach him via his cell phone or e-mail. Then into his bag he threw one pair of slacks and a decent shirt, his travel shaving kit and a bottle of Excedrin.

He called the airport. The first flight anywhere close to Helena wasn't until morning.

Fine.

Tomorrow he'd be off to Whitehorn, Montana, wherever the hell that was. He wouldn't warn the old man that he was coming ahead of time. Nope, he wanted to catch Garrett "Grandpappy" Kincaid off guard.

Trent believed in striking first, blindsiding his opponent. Unfortunately Kincaid had done just that to him. It was now time to turn the tables. From memory, he dialed the number of a private investigator he'd used in the past.

"It's me," the recorder stated. "You know the drill. Leave a message after the tone."

Trent waited, then said, "It's Remmington, again. I still want you to find out whatever you can about Celia O'Hara, the paralegal from L.A., but now I want you to check out a couple of guys from Montana. Garrett Kincaid and his son Larry. They hail from a small town called Whitehorn, somewhere east of Helena, located off Highway 191 near the Laughing Horse Reservation. Find out anything and everything you can about these guys and e-mail me or call me on the cell. Thanks." He hung up, discarded the idea of a second drink, stared at the lightning through the window and waited for dawn.

* * *

As she drove her rented Ford Explorer across the ranch land of western Montana, Gina glanced at her watch and smiled to herself. She was making good time from the airport, and her job was just about finished. She'd helped Garrett Kincaid locate six of his son's illegitimate children. The only question that remained was whether Larry had sired a seventh.

She was willing to bet her life on it. There was that notation in the date book/journal Larry had kept. It read simply, "Found out former flame had baby boy. Check into this. Could be mine. Timing seems perfect." It could have been idle scribbling, but Gina didn't think so; it wasn't Larry's style. No, there was a baby, all right, and she imagined, given Larry's track record for fathering illegitimate sons, the boy was a Kincaid. The date book had been stuffed into the box of Larry's personal effects, the one relating to all of his bastard sons. Gina had a feeling that another child had indeed been born, just in the past year or so, a seventh illegitimate son. Because of Larry's whereabouts in his last year, Gina would bet dollars to donuts that baby was somewhere in the state, probably not too far from the town of Whitehorn. Well, she thought with the determination she was known for, she'd leave no stone unturned to find the kid.

Though she'd never met the man, Gina held a particular dislike for Larry; he'd been the antithesis of his father, Garrett. A hard-drinking, womanizing, gambling man, Larry Kincaid had swaggered through life without a bit of empathy, understanding, or interest in anyone else. He'd fathered illegitimate children as if he were in some kind of contest, then pretty much ignored the offspring as well as the women who had borne them. Garrett, on the other hand, was decent and straitlaced, a man of strict morals, a man as steady and true as Montana, the vast land that had spawned him.

All in all, she'd enjoyed locating Garrett's lost grandsons…well, except for one. The hellion. But she wouldn't think of Trent Remmington now. She'd compromised her own rules when she'd met up with him last month—lying about who she was—and that thought still stuck in her craw.

She'd made a mistake of biblical proportions on that one and nearly lost her heart in the process.

"Fool," she muttered, kicking off her sandals to drive barefoot. She reached into her open handbag sitting on the passenger seat. Squinting, and avoiding a truck speeding in the opposite direction of this long stretch of highway, she dug into her purse, found her sunglasses and managed to slip them out of their case and onto her nose.

A few years ago, just out of college, she'd begged her brother Jack to let her work with him as a private investigator. He'd balked at first, but finally agreed, and she'd sworn then that she would never get involved with any of her clients.

It hadn't been a problem. Until she'd met Trent Remmington.

"Stupid, stupid woman," she berated herself under

her breath as she flipped on the radio. Listening to what little news there was, she leaned an arm out the window and felt the hot May wind pull at the strands of her hair. Acres and acres of rolling ranch land stretched as far as the eye could see under the deep blue Montana sky.

Fences sliced fields spotted with all shapes and colors of cattle and horses. She smiled at the sight of a Brahman calf with its tiny hump mounted over its shoulders and wide, curious eyes watching as she passed. Spotted longhorns ambled along a creek bank and a frisky colt in another field lifted his tail like a banner and ran, kicking its black legs and shaking its head as he joined a small herd of Appaloosas.

The wide expanse was a far cry from the crowded confines of L.A. It was quiet here, maybe too quiet for her, but a nice change of pace. She would only be here awhile. Garrett had invited her to stay at the ranch as she peeked under every as-yet-unturned stone in her search for Larry's baby. She'd decided to take Garrett up on his offer. She'd always wanted to spend a week on a real working ranch, and now it seemed she was going to get her fantasy chance. She wouldn't stay longer than a week; not when she knew that the rest of Larry's brood would show up soon and she'd come face-to-face with Trent Remmington again.

Somehow she was going to avoid that. Though Garrett had been making noises about her sticking around, meeting the sons and explaining her part in finding them all, she was going to politely turn him down.

There was just no reason to stay.

She spied the turnoff to the Kincaid ranch, just as Faith Hill's voice wafted from the speakers. Cranking hard on the wheel, she headed down a long lane of twin ruts. Tall dry grass grew between the parallel trails of sparse gravel, brushing the undercarriage of the car. Potholes and rocks dotted the dusty laneway and Gina smiled at the pure, raw grit of this part of the country. She spied a tractor chugging in one field, and farther ahead, climbing to the sky, craggy mountains spired over rolling, pine-covered foothills.

Gina slowed as the lane curved toward what appeared to be the heart of the spread. Clustered around the perimeter of a hard-packed parking area were the stables, undergoing some kind of renovation, a bunkhouse, and a variety of buildings including a weathered pump house and a variety of machine sheds and the like. The most commanding building of all—despite its disrepair—was a once-stately two-storied ranch house that dominated the parking area. Once beautiful, it was slowly going to seed. Shutters missing slats sagged near the windows, the once-white paint was beginning to peel, and more than one windowpane had been boarded over. A broad porch skirted the first floor and a man was standing on the steps. A tall man with broad shoulders, dark hair and...and—

"Oh, God."

Gina slammed on the brakes and the Explorer shuddered to a stop.

There, big as life—no, make that bigger than life—
was Gina's own personal nightmare.

Trent Remmington was waiting for her.

And, from the looks of him, he was mad as hell.

Two

Gina slowly eased her foot from the brake and shut off the engine. How could this have happened? Trent wasn't supposed to be here until next week.

"Give me strength," she whispered, her palms suddenly damp as they clenched the steering wheel. Through the open sunroof the Montana sun streamed down in what felt like harsh, merciless waves. Heat crawled up the back of her neck and images—a kaleidoscope of dark, seductive pictures—played through her brain. In her mind's eye she saw all too vividly his tanned skin, rippling muscles, bare, broad shoulders and oh, so much more as he lay next to her on the bed in Dallas, kissing her, touching her, making her tingle inside….

Stop it!

Though it was only the middle of May, she was suddenly as hot as if it were late August. She couldn't think of their night together in Dallas. Wouldn't. Gritting her teeth, she reminded herself that she was a grown woman, a private investigator, for crying out loud. She didn't have to feel an ounce of shame or obligation or…or even kid herself that she'd been in love with him. No way. No how.

So why was her stomach doing a slow roll of anticipation at the mere sight of him?

Crossing her fingers, Gina blinked and silently prayed that she was seeing things.

She wasn't.

Trent Remmington was here at the ranch. All six feet, two inches of him. He stood on the front porch of the rambling, two-storied ranch house, his arms folded across his chest, his lips drawn into a thin line of disapproval. His eyes squinted against the bright spring sun, his jaw was set, and the hank of dark hair she'd found so fetching fell across his forehead as he glared at her.

Well, like it or not, she had to deal with him. Now. He would certainly demand answers she wasn't prepared to give. Her feet scrambled into the sandals and for a fleeting second she thought she might have gotten lucky. Maybe the man on the porch wasn't Trent, but his identical twin Blake. That would explain the uncharacteristic jeans and faded denim shirt.

No, she was only kidding herself. She'd researched both brothers. Blake and Trent, though they looked alike, were as different in personality as night and day.

Blake, a pediatrician now living in Southern California, was kindhearted, well-meaning, without the hard edge of his irreverent renegade of a twin. This tough-as-leather man glaring through the dusty, bug-spattered windshield at her was Trent Remmington. No two ways about it. He might have discarded his two-thousand-dollar suit and designer tie, but he still wore the same arrogant attitude of the maverick oilman he was.

To make matters worse, he obviously recognized her. If looks could kill, Gina Henderson, a.k.a. Celia O'Hara, would right now be six feet under and pushing up daisies.

She shoved open the door to the Explorer and stepped out onto sparse gravel. "Give me strength," she whispered to any guardian angel who happened to be passing by. Leaving her briefcase, laptop computer and overnight bags in the car, she forced some starch into her spine as she marched across the lot. She was suddenly aware of her rumpled khaki skirt and sleeveless blouse that she'd thrown on hours ago in L.A. Her lipstick had probably faded and her hair was a tangled mess from the wind that had caught hold of it through the open windows and sunroof of the Explorer, but there wasn't time to repair any of her feminine armor. Not that it mattered, anyway.

An old shaggy dog, with more shepherd than Lab in his gene pool, was lying on a patch of bare ground near the porch. In the shade of a shrub, he gave off a soft "Woof" as she approached.

"It's all right," she told the mutt, though she didn't

believe it for a minute herself. He thumped the ground with his tail and didn't bother climbing to his feet.

She stood in front of the stairs and looked up. "We've got to quit meeting like this," she said to break the ice.

He didn't so much as crack a smile.

She didn't blame him.

"What the hell are you doing here?"

So much for pleasantries.

"Looking for me?" he continued.

"What?" She nearly laughed. If he only knew that she would have run in the other direction if she'd but guessed he was here.

"I don't believe in coincidence." Blue eyes drilled into her.

"Neither do I." His voice brought back memories of laughter and seduction, memories she quickly cast aside. Her smile faded and she cleared her throat as she stared into a square-jawed face branded forever in her brain. "I'm actually here to see Garrett Kincaid."

"You know him?" His eyes narrowed as she reached the bottom stair. Yet he didn't make a step toward her, didn't move, didn't offer the hint of a smile, just stood, jeans-clad legs apart, denim shirt-tails flapping in the honeysuckle-laced breeze, arms folded across that broad expanse of chest she'd known so intimately.

This wasn't the time for lies. "I work for Garrett," she admitted, and could almost see the gears whirring in his mind with this new information.

"You work for him?" he repeated, assessing her all over again.

She mounted the steps and stood close enough to touch him for the first time since ducking out of the DeMarco Hotel five or six weeks ago as the first light of dawn had crept over Dallas. She blushed at the thought of their last meeting, but managed to keep her eyes trained on his.

"He hired me."

"Then I take it you're not a paralegal."

"No," she admitted, wishing she could drop through the battered floorboards. "I'm a private investigator, hired to locate all of Garrett's grandsons."

Deep grooves bracketed his mouth. "Anything else you lied about?"

"Oh, yeah," she admitted, blushing as she nodded and cranked her chin up a couple of notches. "Quite a few things, unfortunately. It, um…" She met his gaze, then looked away in embarrassment. "It seemed appropriate at the time, but… Well, I don't see any reason to beat around the bush now, but I think maybe Garrett should be involved in this conversation."

"Why?"

"This is his gig. He hired me and I don't know what he's already said to you, if anything. There are things he might want to tell you himself."

"I'll bet."

She glanced at the house. "I take it he's not here?"

Trent shook his head and the afternoon sunlight

touched the thick mahogany-dark strands that brushed his collar and tops of his ears. "The foreman said he's gone into town for some supplies."

Wonderful, she thought sarcastically. Now she was stuck here. With Trent and her lies. "But you have met him."

"Not yet." Uncompromising blue eyes appraised her. "He called, invited me to come here next week, and I decided to jump the gun a bit."

No wonder Garrett hadn't warned her that Trent would be here. He hadn't known himself.

"So, you live here in Whitehorn?" Obviously the inquisition wasn't over.

"No," she said quickly. "The L.A. part was the truth."

"What wasn't, Celia?"

She cringed inwardly at the name she'd come up with on the spur of the moment. "For starters, my name is Gina Henderson."

One dark eyebrow cocked, encouraging her to go on. She glanced at the barn where a tractor pulling a trailer piled high with bales of hay had rumbled to a stop. Two ranch hands seated high on the mountain of hay jumped off and began unloading the bales, tossing them onto a conveyer that was positioned to move the bales upward and dump them into an open doorway on the second story of the barn. She could see other workers standing at the ready to stack them in the hay loft.

"Anything else I should know, *Gina?*"

"Oh, yeah, probably a lot, but let's just wait and

Garrett can explain all the sordid, gory details," she suggested, wiping away a drip of sweat that had slid down the side of her face.

"All right. We'll play it your way. But when he gets here, I expect to hear the truth."

"You probably won't like it."

His smile was as cold as a November rain. "I'm sure I won't," he agreed. "I'm damn sure I won't."

"Wait a minute," Jordan Baxter insisted, leaning back in his desk chair and studying his daughter, Hope, with a jaundiced eye. Propping the heel of one polished boot on top of a neat stack of deeds, he narrowed his eyes on the one good thing he'd accomplished in his life. "You're telling me that Garrett Kincaid is gathering all of Larry's bastard children, here in Whitehorn?" His stomach turned at the thought. From the first time Dugin, one of those uppity Kincaid brothers had called him "white trash" back in grade school, Jordan Baxter had hated the whole family.

Hope slapped a file onto the edge of her father's desk and leaned a hip against the corner. "I'm only telling you what I heard down at the Hip Hop Café at lunch today. It's probably not true, anyway."

Jordan hoped she was right. Hip Hop was gossip central in Whitehorn. Some of the information bandied about over elk hash, blueberry pie and hot coffee was right on; the rest was just the talk of bored, small-town minds ready to make a little excitement for themselves.

Hope lifted a slim shoulder as if she didn't care what her father thought. Wearing black slacks and a T-shirt, her wheat-colored hair pulled back in a pony-tail, she looked even younger than her twenty-five years. She was on the naive side, but, given the way her father had protected her over the years, that was to be expected. She was smart as the proverbial whip.

"Six bastards?" he repeated with a long, low whistle. "And all boys?"

Hope offered an indulgent smile. "I'm not sure, Dad. It's just what I heard, and now you're getting all worked up again." She sighed and moved from his desk to lean against the door frame to the outer office. "I shouldn't have said anything." She actually looked as though she regretted confiding in him.

"Listen, honey, this is the kind of thing I need to know. In a small town, fortunes can be made or destroyed by one little bit of information. If it's true. So, who was talking about it—and don't tell me Lily Mae Wheeler. That old battle-ax lives and breathes gossip and none of it's reliable."

"I overheard Janie talking with Winona Cobbs."

"Winona? Well, that explains it." Jordan let out a puff of disgusted air. "With all her psychic mumbo-jumbo, that woman should be locked away instead of being allowed to sell junk on the interstate." He glanced up and saw Hope trying to swallow a smile. "What? You know as well as I do that she acts as if she's been smokin' peyote."

"Janie was the one who had the information. And you'd better be careful, Dad," Hope said, "talk like that about Winona could get you into trouble. It's called slander, I think."

Jordan let his feet fall to the floor. "I just call 'em as I see 'em." But if Janie Austin was passing along the information on the Kincaids, then there might just be some truth woven into the local gossip. Janie usually knew her stuff. Bright and pretty, she had access not only to all the information that was passed from table to table at the Hip Hop Café, but she was married to Reed Austin, the deputy sheriff, who knew just about everything going on in the county. Nope, Janie wasn't someone to create grist for the ever-turning gossip mill of Whitehorn.

So it could be true.

Whitehorn might be about to have a huge influx of Kincaids.

Stomach acid burned in Jordan's esophagus and he reached into his desk drawer for a package of Rolaids tablets to help with the heartburn. He shoved back his chair. "I guess I'll just have to check this out myself."

"You do that," Hope advised as she returned to her desk in the reception area.

Jordan grabbed his hat and caught his reflection in the mirror mounted near the door. At forty-six he was a long way from over the hill, but the silver in his dark hair and the lines around his eyes and mouth reminded him that he wasn't getting any younger. He exercised regularly, was fit, didn't even have the hint of a gut, but the years were beginning to show. He'd hate to think how many of those gray hairs and wrinkles were the direct result of dealing with those damned Kincaids. That family had been the bane of his existence all his life and the thought that there were six more heretofore-unknown brothers about to appear in Whitehorn did nothing to improve his mood.

"Don't forget that Jeremiah Kincaid killed your grandmother," he said, passing his daughter's desk.

Hope rolled her eyes. "C'mon, Dad, that isn't fair. The coroner said she drank too much and was smoking in bed. That's what caused the fire, not some devious plot by the Kincaid family. You're the only person in the entire State of Montana who thinks Jeremiah was behind it."

"He was." The bastard. Rich, powerful, and deadly, he'd taken Vera Baxter to his bed, then cut her free. When she wouldn't accept his rejection, she'd ended up dead in a conflagration that Jordan didn't believe she caused for a minute.

"Does it matter? They're both dead now. Let it go."

"I'll think about it," he lied, as his fists clenched in frustration. Slowly he straightened his fingers. He wanted to argue, to bring up every incident where a Kincaid had screwed over a Baxter, so that his daughter would understand the legacy of pain every Baxter had borne, but he didn't. Hope wouldn't believe him, anyway. She was just too damned naive for her own good.

"I hope you're wrong about this," he said, straightening his tie.

"Me, too." She held his gaze for a second. "I don't want to see you get all crazy about it."

"I won't." Well, not crazy, but his blood did curdle at the thought of even one more Kincaid in the area. Jeremiah had been a half cousin to Garrett, or something like that. The way those Kincaids screwed around it was hard keeping 'em all straight. Not that he really wanted to.

"So, Larry fathered six kids out of wedlock. It figures." He chuckled without a hint of mirth as he squared his hat on his head and reached for the doorknob. "I bet that just about killed Garrett when he found out."

"The way Lily Mae tells it, Garrett's planning to divide up the Whitehorn ranch among the heirs. To make amends or something."

That stopped him short. He let the doorknob go, and faced his daughter. "I thought you said Janie Austin had the information."

"She did, but Lily Mae put her two cents in."

Jordan's back teeth ground together as he thought of the Kincaid ranch—the place where he'd worked his tail off as a kid, the ranch that had been promised to him. "You know that spread is supposed to be mine. Ours. It used to be called the Baxter place before the Kincaids swindled it from us."

Hope sighed and a sadness settled in her eyes. Once

again he felt an incredible urge to protect her, for she was the light of his life.

"Why don't you give it up, Dad?" she asked. "What's your fascination with the Kincaid place, anyway? I know when Uncle Cameron owned the ranch he promised it to you, but that was years ago. And you've got so much already."

That much was true. Jordan had made his own fortune years ago working for an investment firm in New York. Young, fresh out of college, and determined to put his poor roots behind him, he'd taken to investment banking like a fish to water. But his roots were here. In Whitehorn. Though he now owned thousands of acres in the county, none meant anything to him. The old Baxter place did. When times had been tough, it had been his home. He felt a lump rise in his throat and steadfastly swallowed it back.

"You know, Dad, you could buy and sell a dozen places around here. All of them would put the Kincaid ranch to shame."

"It's not about money, darlin'," he said, wishing his only child understood, but then, she hadn't experienced the grinding poverty he had, nor endured the taunts from some of the wealthier kids in Whitehorn that he'd heard while growing up. The worst had been the disparaging remarks and mean-spirited gibes that had been cast his way by the Kincaid boys. "Nope, it's not about money at all, Hope," he repeated, his voice a little rough. "It's about pride. Family pride. That's all that matters in this world and it's time you knew it."

* * *

"When did you say Garrett was due back?" Gina asked, wondering how she could possibly make small talk with this man.

"I didn't. The foreman—"

"Rand Harding," she said automatically.

Trent nodded. "He wasn't sure, but didn't think it would be long."

Gina mentally crossed her fingers. The less time alone she had with Trent, the better.

"So, I guess this would be a good time for you and I to get to know each other," he suggested, resting a hip against the railing. "If I recall correctly, we have some unfinished business between us."

More than you know, she thought, her mouth suddenly desert dry. She decided it would be best to keep her secret to herself. Until she was certain.

"You're talking about Dallas." Her heart kicked into overdrive as she thought about that night. He stared at her so hard she found it difficult to take a breath. Oh, Lord, why wasn't she immune to him? Why hadn't she forgotten him after that one star-spangled night they'd shared? Why was she such an idiot where he was concerned? "I don't think we should go into that."

"Why not?"

Unspoken accusations fairly crackled in the warm spring air. "Because there's no point to it. We had a night together, it was a mistake, and that's the end of it."

He grabbed her arm as if he expected her to flee. "Not exactly the end. We're both here now."

"So we are," she said, wishing she was anyplace else on earth other than standing toe-to-toe with him, sandal to scruffy boot, feeling his work-roughened fingertips on her skin and smelling the faint seductive scent of the aftershave he'd been wearing when she'd first met him. For a second she thought he might kiss her the way he had in Dallas. Her throat caught and it took all her strength to yank her arm free of him. "But I don't think we need to go into all that."

Thankfully, the old dog ambled up the steps to lay at her feet. "Some watchdog you are," she said, grateful for an excuse to not stare into Trent's silently accusing eyes. She reached down and scratched the mutt behind his ears. His dark eyes regarded her warmly, a wet, pink tongue slid out of the side of his mouth and he rolled over, offering her his belly to be rubbed.

"Seems like you've made a friend for life," Trent observed.

And right now I need each and every one, she thought.

The sound of a truck engine reached Gina's ears and she turned to see a big pickup lumbering down the lane. Piled high with sacks of grain, the bed sat low over the tires. Behind the wheel, aviator sunglasses in place, was Garrett Kincaid, the patriarch of a brood of six, maybe even seven, illegitimate grandchildren. Gina had never actually met any of the grown men and women who had Kincaid blood running through their veins.

Except for Trent.

And that meeting had proved a disaster of monumental proportions. In his case—and in his case only—she had let her personal curiosity overcome her self-imposed rule to distance herself from her clients.

"See, now, you didn't have to wait so long, after all," Trent said sarcastically. "Let's go have a chat with Gramps, shall we?"

He grabbed her wrist, making her pulse jump. With long, ground-eating strides he half dragged her as he made his way toward the stables where Garrett had parked beneath a solitary pine tree.

"Just wait a minute," she said as she jogged to keep up with him. She jerked her arm free. "I, um, I think it would be best if Garrett didn't know anything about what happened between you and me in Dallas," she admitted, feeling her cheeks stain with color that had nothing to do with the intensity of the sun. He didn't say a word, just waited, eyes narrowed, cords at the back of his neck standing out above the sun-bleached collar of his shirt.

"He wouldn't approve?"

"It's not that, but—"

"Don't worry about me, darlin'. I'm not the kind to kiss and tell." Trent's smile was pure saccharine.

She felt like a damned fool. "Good, because what happened between us had nothing to do with you being Garrett's grandson. You're the only one I ever met and…well…" She let her voice trail off; there was just no reason to go into it any further.

"Only one. You mean, you didn't meet Blake?"

She nodded. "Nor any of the other brothers."

He froze. "'Other brothers'?"

She hesitated. "Garrett didn't tell you?"

His jaw slid to one side. "Why don't you?"

In for a penny, in for a pound, she supposed. He'd learn soon enough. "Larry Kincaid fathered six sons out of wedlock, quite possibly seven."

Trent's eyes narrowed suspiciously. "Are you trying to tell me that, besides me and my twin, there are five others? That I've got five half brothers?"

"Well, actually, you have six half brothers, excluding your twin, and a half sister. Larry had a son, Collin, and daughter, Melanie, with his wife Sue Ellen. The rest were the result of his affairs with several different women."

Trent stared at her as if she'd gone mad. "That's impossible," he said as the conveyer loading the hay bales rumbled and a calf in a nearby field bawled plaintively. "No one's that stupid. Not in this day and age."

"It would be better for Garrett to explain this," she said, realizing she'd said too much. "He can tell you about your father."

"Let's get one thing straight," he said slowly, his nostrils flaring just a bit as he leaned down to drill her with those incredible blue eyes. "Larry Kincaid is *not* my father. It takes a helluva lot more than a one-night stand for a man to earn that title."

"I suppose." She swallowed hard at the irony in his words.

He glanced to the parking area near the stables where

Garrett was climbing out of his truck. "And as for what happened in Dallas, I'll keep it to myself. For now."

"Good."

"Now I think it's time to get a few things straight with the old man." With that he strode toward the truck and left Gina behind, feeling like an utter fool.

Trent zeroed in on the man who claimed to be his grandfather as the older man walked around a dented fender of the truck.

"You must be Trent." Garrett removed his sunglasses, stuffed them into a pocket of his faded plaid shirt and extended his hand. "Here a bit early, aren't you?"

"I guess I just couldn't wait."

"Fair enough." Garrett's smile was rock-steady. "Glad to finally meet you. Sorry it took so long."

Trent took the older man's hand. Garrett's clasp was strong and sure, his face weathered, his straight hair nearly silver. There was a trace of Native American in him, the coppery skin and high cheekbones giving testament to it, but his eyes were a startling blue. Intense enough that, Trent guessed, they could cut through any amount of bull slung in the old man's direction. "So, what do I call you? Gramps?" He couldn't hide the sarcasm in his tone. Trent had learned long ago not to rely on family. A man made his own way in the world. Period. He relied on no one.

"Garrett will do."

"Good."

"I guess I should start out by apologizing for my son." Pain stole through the old man's eyes. "I had no

"I already talked to Rand. He showed me up to a room at the main house. He seemed to think it would be okay with you." Trent glanced at the two-storied home sitting upon a slight rise.

"More than okay. Just as long as you're all settled in."

"For a while," Trent said. He scratched his forearm and asked a question that had been bothering him. "I suppose you contacted Blake?"

"Yes. Talked to him this morning. Said he'd give you a call."

"I guess he missed me."

"And you didn't call him?"

"No."

Trent shook his head and didn't elaborate as he, along with Garrett, walked Gina to her Explorer. No reason to get into his problems with his twin right now. He had a feeling it would all come out soon enough.

"Blake will be here next week," Garrett said as Gina opened the back of her car. "So will the others."

Trent was faced with half a dozen bags. This lady didn't know the meaning of traveling light. "A regular family reunion." Trent pulled out a medium-size bag.

"Or irregular," Garrett corrected.

Trent's eyes narrowed as he considered the man who had sired him. "Eight kids by six different women. Didn't Larry know anything about birth control?"

"I guess not." Garrett scowled as he grabbed a bag. "And I'd say it's damned lucky for you that he didn't."

Three

Gina dropped her suitcase onto the bed and mentally kicked herself from one side of the sparse room to the other. Trent Remmington—why was he the one who'd shown up unannounced? What kind of cruel irony was that? Any of the other heirs she could have dealt with, but not Trent. Not until she was ready to face him again…and then again, maybe not ever. But all that had changed.

She hung up her few dresses in a closet about the size of a coffin, then refolded several pairs of jeans and T-shirts and placed them in a tall oak bureau. Glancing at her reflection in the cracked oval mirror attached to the bureau, she saw the wild state of her hair and the remainder of what had once been her makeup.

"Great," she groaned. She was cranky and out of

sorts—probably just because she'd had to face Trent again. Certainly there was no other reason, right?

Biting her lower lip, she touched her tight, flat abdomen.

Was it possible? Could she be pregnant? Seeing Trent again only reinforced her worries. She'd never been one of those women whose menstrual cycle was like clockwork, but even she was overdue for her period.

"It's just your nerves," she said, picking up her brush and working it through the tangles in her hair. "This case has got you in knots."

But she wasn't convinced as she twisted her hair and pinned it with a clip, then applied a fresh sheen of lipstick and called it good. Sighing, she sat on the edge of the narrow bed and wondered how long she could stand to call this room her home. A sun-faded rug covered the wood floor and a small desk, shoved into a corner, doubled as a nightstand. The room smelled faintly musty, so she threw open a window, letting in a breeze that billowed ancient lace curtains.

From her vantage point on the second story, she watched the old dog sniff his way to an oak tree where he stopped to eye a squirrel scrambling in the overhead branches. On the other side of the fence, sedate mares grazed in one pasture, their coats shining in the sun while spindly legged foals frolicked and scampered, sending up puffs of dust. Not far off, in a field so large she couldn't see the fence line, a herd of cattle lumbered along the banks of a creek that sliced through the lush grassland.

Gina wondered about the men and women who lived here, so far from a large city. She watched as Garrett and a strapping man in a cowboy hat and dusty jeans unloaded the sacks of feed from the back of the pickup. The conveyer had stopped moving and one of the hands had hopped back onto the tractor. With a growl and plume of black smoke, the old John Deere headed through an open gate.

Horses nickered, cattle lowed, and a wasp buzzed as it worked hard on a muddy nest hanging just under the eaves. Gina inhaled the fresh air laced with the scents of spring flowers and new-mown hay, then sighed.

"Heaven on earth," she heard, and whipped around to find Trent standing in the doorway, one shoulder propped insolently against the jamb, his arms folded across his chest.

"Looks like it."

"Even to a city girl?"

"Especially to a city girl."

To her surprise, he strode into the room and swung the door shut behind him. "I think we'd better talk," he said, grabbing the desk chair. He swung it around backward, straddled the seat and leaned his arms across the back. "You start."

"By?"

"By telling me what's going on. With the old man, with you—whoever you are. Let's start with Dallas."

"That was a mistake," she said, meeting his gaze evenly. "I think we both know it."

"It wasn't a setup?"

"Excuse me? A setup? What…?" She stared into his angry blue eyes and suddenly understood. "You think I planned meeting you and…and what?"

"Seducing me."

She nearly laughed. The man was out of his ever-lovin' mind. "Don't flatter yourself, Remmington. I'd had too much to drink, so had you. I had no idea you'd be in that hotel bar that night and—"

"And you knew who I was. An advantage, I'd say."

"It wasn't a game."

"No?" He scowled and rubbed his chin. "Sure feels like one now. One that I somehow lost." His gaze drilled deep into hers. "Believe it or not, I'm not used to losing."

The man was damned irritating, but someone she had to deal with, like it or not. "I understand."

"That's right. You know all about me." He stood and crossed the few feet separating them, looming over her to the point that she nearly backed into the open window, but somehow stood her ground. "And I know nothing about you, do I?"

"Except what I've told you."

"Exactly. So let's get one very important thing straight, shall we? I don't like anyone snooping into my life. Period. And I don't trust people who lie to me. So you already have two strikes against you in this little 'non-game.' The way I see it, three strikes and you're out."

She told herself not to lose it. To grab on to the rags of her temper and hold tight. But she couldn't. It wasn't her nature. "Look, Trent—I can call you that, right, considering the circumstances. 'Mr. Remmington' seems a little formal. Yes, I was hired by Garrett to find you, not to pry into your personal life, but to locate you and determine that you were one of Larry Kincaid's sons. That's all. I lied to you that night in Dallas because I—I—"

"Didn't want to blow your cover?"

"Well, yeah, that's kind of a TV-cop way of describing it, but I'd told myself I wasn't going to meet any of the Kincaid heirs, that I would keep this as professional as possible and then…okay, I blew it. I have to confess, when I stumbled into you that night and you started flirting with me, I couldn't resist. I guess you're just too damned irresistible. Is that what you wanted to hear?"

He stared at her as if he couldn't believe a word. Neither could she, but she couldn't stop herself and she was far from finished.

"So, in answer to your question—" she closed the gap between them to mere inches and glared up at him as if she wasn't shaking inside "—meeting you wasn't part of some nefarious scheme or shakedown or whatever you want to call it. It was, as I said before, a mistake. Maybe it's one that we should just get over, okay?"

A huge hand snaked forward to clamp possessively over her forearm. "Get over? I don't know about you, lady, but that kind of thing doesn't happen to me every day of the week."

"Oh, save me." She glanced down at the hand encircling her arm. "And remove that now. I'm not going for any of your Neanderthal tactics."

His fingers released and she walked around him, picked up her laptop computer case and unzipped it. "Was there anything else you wanted to grill me about?" she asked, glancing over her shoulder as she placed the sleek little computer on the desk near her bed.

"I just wanted to clear the air."

"Consider it cleared." She found the outlet and plugged in her machine, then, ignoring the drumming of her heart, looked around for a phone jack.

As if he understood her dilemma, he said, "There aren't any connections in the rooms. I already checked." With a thumb hooked toward the wall, he added, "I'm in the next room."

Her stomach tightened. He was close, too damned close. Just one door down the hall? In a house that had seven bedrooms. Just…great.

"I've already talked to Garrett and placed a call to the local phone company to have a few more lines installed, but it'll take a while." He walked to the door and swung it wide, then strode through and said over his shoulder, "As I said earlier, 'This ain't exactly L.A.'"

So it was true, Jordan thought as he shoved his plate to one side of the table. He'd eaten a long, late lunch, listening to the gossip buzzing around him like a swarm of mosquitoes on a stagnant swamp. Garrett Kincaid had, with the help of a private investigative firm from

somewhere in California, located Larry's illegitimate
brood. He'd also managed to get control of the ranch
that Jordan considered his own private legacy. Of
course, he'd been screwed out of it. All those promises
his uncle Cameron had made weren't diddly squat.
Once again, the Kincaids had kicked the Baxters.

Hell.

Frowning darkly, Jordan stirred his coffee and his blood
boiled, but he somehow managed to hold his tongue. He'd
learned a long time ago it was better to get even than to
get mad, but that took considerable self-control.

Jordan took a long sip from his cup, eyed the desserts
that were slowly cooling in a rotating display case, and
eased back in his booth. He was alone, which was
fitting, he supposed. Since returning to Whitehorn a
millionaire several times over, he'd collected a lot of
"friends," but he didn't trust any of them. He knew they
only liked him for his money and what he could do for
them. Yep, he was becoming a powerful man here in
Whitehorn and he'd been feeling pretty good about
himself until Wayne Kincaid hadn't accepted his offer
to buy back the ranch he should have inherited.

"How about a piece of pie?" Janie asked, dragging
him out of his vengeful thoughts. She was a cute thing
and efficient as all get-out. Her blond hair was pulled
back into a ponytail and her perennial smile was tacked
neatly in place. Head waitress and would-be manager,
she ran the Hip Hop Café these days. "We've got fresh
strawberry-rhubarb, and isn't that your favorite?"

"Yep, but I think I'll pass."

"Your loss," she teased, and refilled his cup.

"Hey, what's this I hear about Garrett Kincaid buying the ranch from Wayne and fillin' it up with the grandkids that Larry left all over the country?"

Little lines formed between Janie's eyebrows and she hesitated. She wasn't one prone to gossip, unlike most of her clientele. "That's the word. I haven't talked to Garrett myself about it, though, so, I guess it's still just hearsay." She slapped Jordan's check onto the table as the front door opened and a group of teenagers walked in. "If you reconsider about the pie, flag me down."

"Will do." He reached for his wallet and eyed the crowd. There was Lily Mae, the town's premier gossip, dressed to kill, as usual, in a tight lavender sweater and matching slacks. At another table Winona Cobbs's graying head was ducked low as she engaged Christina Montgomery, the mayor's younger daughter, in a quiet conversation.

From different tables of the packed café he heard the name Kincaid mentioned several times.

"Six of 'em, can you believe it?" Lily Mae was saying. "All with different mothers, aside from the twins, that is." She was spouting off to a woman Jordan didn't recognize. "And there's talk of another one. I tell you, say what you will about Larry Kincaid, he was certainly a charmer."

Jordan snorted and finished his coffee.

He'd heard enough. Larry Kincaid's bastard sons

were about to descend upon the town. He left several bills, including a healthy tip, and tossed his napkin onto the table. That's just what the town needed. More Kincaids, and bastards at that.

Well, really, he thought bitterly as he jaywalked, dodging a sports car that was speeding down Center Avenue, weren't they all?

Why did he let the woman get to him? Trent wondered as he helped unload a sack of feed and stacked it in the stables. So she'd sneaked around, so she'd lied to him, so he hadn't been able to resist her that one hot night in Dallas. So what? Forget her. He just had to put up with her for a few days here in Whitehorn and then he'd fly out and leave her forever.

Right?

He gritted his teeth and using his body, slammed the sacks of feed nearer the wall, straightening each stack. He tried to ignore the feeling that Gina was different, that she wasn't just the love-'em-and-leave-'em kind of woman he associated with one-night stands. His jaw clamped tight. Years ago he hadn't thought one way or the other about meeting a woman and bedding her. But as he'd aged, he'd become more selective, more careful, restraining himself. He'd learned that people, women included, always wanted something from him, something more than he was willing to give.

So he'd been cautious. Until that damned night in Dallas.

"Something wrong?" Garrett asked as he dragged

the last sack from the truck and flung it on top of the pile. For an old man he was strong, a hard worker, though Trent did detect a hint of a limp and glimpsed the sweat that ran down the back of his neck. Garrett yanked off his battered leather gloves and set them on top of a barrel of oats. "You look like something's eating at you."

"Got a lot to think about."

"Don't we all?" Together they strode through the fading sunlight to the main house. They kicked off their boots on the back porch and walked into the kitchen where a pretty woman with dark upswept hair was over-seeing boiling pots on the stove and peering into the oven. "The chicken's about done," she said, looking up at Garrett with dark, shining eyes. "I'll just whip these potatoes and you can gather in the dining room. Oh, hi." She spied Trent, wiped a hand on her apron and extended it. "I'm Suzanne."

"Rand's wife," Garrett said quickly. "My grandson, Trent Remmington. I called Suzanne in to pinch-hit with the cooking until I can find someone to take over. Suzanne, here, is an accountant in town."

"That is when I'm not playing Julia Child," she teased, then laughed at the pseudo-consternation twisting Garrett's features.

"Actually, I don't mind," she said as she found a couple of pot holders and carried a kettle of boiled potatoes to the sink. She poured most of the water down the drain, saving a little in a smaller bowl. "Since my baby, Joe, was born, my career's slowed down. I just do

the books for a few people now. There." She set the pot
of potatoes on the counter and, opening the oven door,
retrieved a couple of golden-brown chickens. "I'll make
the gravy, then serve up in about fifteen minutes. After
that I'd better hurry home. I left Joe with my brother."
She rolled her eyes and grinned.

"Mack's a good kid, but there's only so much 'quality
time' he can stand with his nephew." She laughed brightly
at the thought. "He's seventeen and all thumbs around the
baby, but I figure it's time he learned about kids before
he gets wrapped up in some girl and has one of his own."

"Best form of birth control there is," Trent observed.

Suzanne's smile slid away and Garrett's expression
turned sober. "We'd better wash up."

Realizing the old man was apparently having trouble
with his son's indiscretions, Trent didn't say anything
else. He walked through a long hallway to the main
stairs but at the archway leading to the living room, his
footsteps slowed. He heard Gina's muffled voice.

"I said I'd be back as soon as this was finished, Jack,"
she said hotly, then paused for a few seconds while the
guy on the other end of the line had his say. "Yeah, I
know, I know. I'll wrap this up as soon as I can."

Another pause.

Trent told himself to move on, that she deserved some
privacy, but then he reminded himself that she hadn't
been all that interested in preserving his. For all he knew,
she'd dug into the most intimate details of his life.

And didn't you try to do the same to her? Didn't you

hire a private investigator to find Celia O'Hara and when that didn't pan out, have him look into Garrett Kincaid's life?

He ignored the attack of sudden conscience.

"I'm not sure, Jack," Gina said with a long-suffering sigh. "I'm still looking into it. But I'll be back soon, I promise." She laughed then, that deep, throaty laugh that had caught his attention in Dallas, and he felt a moment of jealousy. "Yeah, I miss you, too… Oh, come on, you know I do. What? …Now, listen, quit worrying! I can take care of myself." He must've said something incredibly amusing again because this time she chuckled. "Fine, I'll remember. If I'm not gonna be back in a couple of days, then you'll just have to carry on without me, and yes, I'm sure it'll break your heart, but believe me, Jack, you can handle it." She listened again, then sighed theatrically. "Me, too. Okay, I've gotta run. I'll call again." Another minute's hesitation while the guy on the other end of the telephone line said his goodbyes. "Love you, too," she said as she hung up.

Trent, feeling like the eavesdropper he was, considered climbing the stairs and high-tailing it to his room. But that seemed a little sneaky and he'd always prided himself on being a straight shooter.

Jamming his fists into his pockets, he sauntered into the living room and found her nestled in the corner of a floral couch that had seen better days, staring at the cold grate of the fireplace. "Boyfriend?" he asked, startling her.

"What?"

He pointed at the phone. "I overheard the tail end of your conversation with your boyfriend. Sounds like he's missing you."

A smile tugged at the corner of those full lips. "Oh, he is." She nodded, her green eyes flashing with amusement, as if she'd just pulled a fast one on him.

"Special guy?" He couldn't help but ask and tried to ignore another jab of unlikely jealousy.

"Very." He could see the pride in the way she held her head. She cared about the man very much. Sunlight pierced the windows and caught in the fiery strands of her hair.

"Known him long?"

"All my life."

That bothered Trent. This guy Jack had watched her grow up while he'd only met her a few weeks earlier. "So, he's kind of a boy next door?"

"You could say that." She was more than amused now, he thought. Curled up on the faded sofa, her bare feet tucked beneath her, a notepad on her lap, she looked cozy and warm, as if she belonged in this rambling old house with its out-of-date, yellowed wallpaper and odd collection of memorabilia. There were all manner of guns mounted on the walls, antlers and animal heads, trophies from long-ago kills now collecting dust in the den and even, down one hallway, a showcase of old Western costumes and Native American paraphernalia.

Trent walked to the fireplace. "This guy—Jack,"

he said, nodding toward the phone. "Does he know about me?"

"He's heard of you, yes."

"About Dallas?"

She blushed and shook her head. "Nope. And I hope he never finds out." She set her notebook aside, hesitated, and finally said, "I thought we were going to let what happened go."

"Can you?"

She bit her lip. All hint of amusement left her face. "I don't know," she said, and it was the first statement she'd made that he believed. "But I'm going to try. Hard. It might be difficult the next couple of days since we'll both be here, but I'm going to see if I can rise above it." Her eyes narrowed a bit. "That is, if you would quit throwing it up in my face. You know, it wasn't as if what happened was all my fault. As the old saying goes, 'it takes two to tango.'"

"But one of us didn't lie about it."

"So flog me with a dozen cat-o'-nine-tails, or toss me in the pillory, or blaze my shirt with a scarlet A...or, oh—" She snapped her fingers and shot to her feet. "I know something even better! Why don't you keep bringing it up and trying to throw some guilt on me, huh? How about that?" With that she turned on a bare heel and stormed out.

He started after her and she sent him a look over one stiff shoulder that was guaranteed to freeze mercury. "Don't, okay? Don't run after me, don't say anything more, and next time I'm on the phone, don't put a glass to the window or listen at the keyhole. It's really none of your business."

"That's where you're wrong, darlin'," he drawled. "You were the one who started poking into my life. Remember? Not the other way around. So I think whatever you do here just might be my business."

"Just stay out of my way."

"That might be impossible."

"Give it a try, okay?" She was out of the room and up the stairs like a shot.

Trent wondered where a man kept his whiskey around this house, and cringed when he heard Suzanne Harding call, "Okay, dinner's on. Come and get it."

Garrett had no idea what had gotten into Trent and Gina, but he didn't like it. No, he didn't like it one bit. All through Suzanne's tasty meal of chicken, mashed potatoes and gravy, applesauce and green beans, they'd both picked at their food, tried their damnedest to ignore one another, and forced smiles onto faces that were both strained and drawn.

Something was up.

If he didn't know better, he'd think they were having themselves some kind of lover's spat. For that's sure what it looked like. But that was impossible. They hardly knew each other.

Trent, shoving his plate aside, finally said, "Okay, so tell me about these other 'brothers' that I've got. How'd you find out about me and them?"

Garrett pushed his chair back from the long table and walked the few steps to the sideboard where Suzanne had left a pot of coffee. Filling three cups, he set them on the table and said, "I was going to explain all this to everyone at the same time, but being as you're here now, I guess I may as well get down to it." He settled into his chair again, felt a pinch of arthritis in his hip and ignored it. This was the tough part, trying to explain his only son's irresponsible actions. "Let's go outside, and sit on the back porch."

Though the two hadn't said a civil word to each other all night, they followed Garrett through French doors to a picnic table and benches. Gina took a seat at the table with Garrett. Trent stood on the porch, bracing his back against a pillar that supported the roof.

"Okay, so shoot," Trent suggested.

Garrett cradled his cup in his hands. This was the hard part. Trying to explain about his son. It pained him. When Larry had been born more than fifty years ago, Garrett had been proud enough to pop. A son. A healthy, good-looking, robust boy. But as the years had passed, Larry had proven to be wayward and ornery, selfish and lazy. Even worse, he'd never been able to keep his hands off women, even as a teenager. But that had been a long time ago.

"This isn't easy, you see. Burying a child, no matter how difficult he was, is painful." Garrett frowned and stared into the dark depths of his coffee. "When Larry died, it about killed me," he admitted, acknowledging that black hole in his heart. "It hadn't been long after Laura had passed away and I was just thankful that she wasn't alive." His lips folded over his teeth and he tamped down the pain that was always with him when he thought of his wife and firstborn. "Anyway, I went through all of Larry's things after he died and I found a safe-deposit box key for a local bank. Larry had asked me to sign on the box years ago and I'd forgotten about it. When I opened it, I discovered a letter from Larry to me or Collin—"

"Who is his legitimate son?" Trent guessed.

"Right. Anyway, there was a smaller box inside the one in the bank and the most important document in that was a letter that explained about the other kids Larry had fathered." He lifted one hand. "There were names, dates, and some addresses, pictures and canceled checks, notes, baby photos, birth certificates…even copies of old report cards. He must've kept everything he ever laid his hands on, and I guess he kept it in the safe-deposit box so when he died someone in the family would know about you and your brothers."

"Thoughtful of him," Trent said sarcastically.

"It was something. Not much, I'll grant you that," Garrett admitted, wishing there was some way he could defend his son. "But at least I found out about you."

"No one else knew about us?"

"Just the mothers, near as I can figure, and they all kept their mouths shut."

"Why?"

"I don't know."

"Some of them were paid," Gina said.

"You're trying to tell me they bribed him or they were given hush money? Is that it?"

Gina lifted a shoulder.

"Who knows," Garrett said. "I didn't figure I should bother them. It's between them and their boys."

Trent let out a snort of disdain. "This family exceeds the limits of dysfunctional." He tossed the rest of his coffee onto the parched grass.

"Then I guess it's time we fixed that."

"Or maybe it's too late."

"Well, I guess we won't know until we try, now, will we?" Garrett asked as Trent cast Gina one last look and strode inside.

Gina attempted to act disinterested but Garrett had been around enough men and women in his life to recognize when two people were interested in each other. In Trent and Gina's case, they were way beyond interested.

Gina had admitted to meeting Trent in Dallas.

Garrett wondered what had happened. But he didn't ask. He figured he might just be better off not knowing.

Four

So much for the quiet of the country lulling her to sleep. Gina tossed off the covers in her tiny bed and padded barefoot across the room to grab her robe—a short cotton thing that worked better as a beach cover-up but was lightweight and easy to pack. Without making a sound, she walked downstairs and out the back door. The moon rode high in an inky sky littered with millions of stars—more stars than she'd ever seen.

Wrapping her arms around her, she hurried along a well-worn path to the stables and there, leaning over the fence railing, she watched the dark shapes of the horses shifting in the night. The air was warm, a light breeze dancing across the fresh-mown hay and playing in the overhead branches of a pine tree.

Peaceful. Serene. Panoramic. So different from the bustle of L.A., a city that was filled with the hum of traffic, beep of keyless locks and scream of sirens at all hours of the night. Here, the chirp of crickets, croak of frogs and occasional nicker from the horses were the only obstructions to a pure, almost ethereal silence.

And Trent Remmington was sleeping in the room next to hers at the main house. Unbelievable! Her fingers tightened over the top rail. So much for tranquility or peace of mind. How had she been so stupid as to get involved with him—if that's what you'd call it. Crueler tongues might dub what had happened between them as a one-night stand or a bar pickup.

She flinched inwardly at the terms. She'd never been one to get involved easily, and, if any name had been fitting for her, it had been Ice Princess as she'd always had a hands-off attitude toward men. At least during the first few dates. She'd grown up watching her divorced mother struggle to make ends meet and eventually marry a man for financial security. Gina had decided then and there that it wasn't a path she'd ever take. No way. No how. Not for her. She would never sacrifice her happiness nor her self esteem for a man—any man—and so, she'd never found one that had really interested her.

Until Trent. Blast the man. She'd been intrigued with Trent Remmington from the first time she'd opened Larry Kincaid's box of memorabilia. The "bad twin," Trent had been as rebellious and wild as his brother Blake had been good and conscientious. Trent drank, smoked, rode motorcycles, boats and horses at breakneck speeds and had the citations, bruises, and scars to prove it.

He'd gone through baby-sitters and governesses like water, even managed to get kicked out of more than one boarding school. When Gina had read his profile, she'd been instantly attracted to the sexy, irreverent rebel. At fifteen he'd "borrowed" an idling bus and tried to drive it through the drive-in window of a local burger hut. At sixteen he'd jumped on a boxcar and rode across the country. At seventeen he'd climbed the ivy-enshrouded halls of his exclusive boarding school to steal a test and been expelled. A few years later, after dropping out of college, he'd bluffed his way through a high-stakes poker game to win. He'd put up the title of his sports car and had come out not only still owning the car—he had still owed Blake the five thousand dollars he'd borrowed for it—but also with the deed to a scrap of property on which he'd eventually discovered oil.

So the hellion who had come within a hair's breadth of landing in jail had ended up a wildcat oilman who had struck it rich without benefit of a higher education or a grandfather or a father to grease the way for him. He'd made his millions by luck, grit and brains.

Trent had not only been strapping, good-looking and blessed with a killer smile, he had also been a child lost, a hellion of a teenager, and a man who, against all odds, had made good.

In retrospect, Gina decided on this starry night, she'd

been well-primed, ready to fall victim to his very serious set of charms.

It had been a night not much different from this one when she'd chanced to run into him. She'd had one last night in Dallas where she'd located Trent Remmington at a convention. Having already checked out his Houston-based corporation, Black Gold International, she'd come to Dallas and got a glimpse of the man himself. Gina had been ready to return to L.A. where Jack was waiting for her to wrap up this case, but, suddenly feeling in the mood for celebration she'd gone downstairs to the patio bar for a glass of wine.

She'd drunk two glasses of wine in less than an hour. Which wasn't so bad, except for the fact that having not eaten since breakfast, the Cabernet had immediately gone to her head. Seated at a table near a planter, she looked across the dance floor toward the bar and spied none other than the object of her most recent hunt: Trent Remmington.

To him, she was a stranger, but from months of re-searching his life, she felt as if she already knew him. She'd spent weeks tracking him down and piecing together his life as the fifth illegitimate son of Larry Kincaid. She'd seen pictures of him, read every article ever written about him, been fascinated by him.

On this spring night she couldn't help but stare as he sipped what looked like a Scotch and water. When he'd glanced her way, she'd dropped her eyes and decided to leave before she did something stupid like introduce herself to him.

She started to leave, but before she could sign off on her tab, the waiter appeared with another glass of wine. "Compliments of the gentleman at the bar."

Her stomach dropped to the floor. She didn't have to look to know that he meant Trent, who, though not staring at her directly, was viewing her in a beveled mirror suspended above the bar.

This is a mistake, she told herself, but managed to smile at the waiter and accept the drink. She glanced at Trent again and, heart knocking ridiculously, held the glass aloft and mouthed, "Thanks."

He nodded, but remained on his bar stool, nursing his drink. A live band tuned up in the corner and a few brave couples, some with incredible dance skills, took over the floor. Gina finished her wine, felt a little light-headed and was about to leave when another glass of Cabernet appeared.

"Oh, no, I couldn't," she said, shaking her head.

"The gentleman insists."

"But—" She started to argue, but the waiter breezed away, taking an order at a nearby table, and Gina was left with the drink. She didn't have to drive, only had to make it up to her room where she'd already asked for a wake-up call, but she didn't need another glass of wine. Didn't want one.

She looked over to the bar and Trent was assessing her, his blue eyes bright in the reflection of the mirror. There was amusement in his gaze, the hint of a smile toying with his lips, and she felt an instant surge of anger.

He was getting off watching her try to decline the stupid glass of wine. And what would happen if she downed it? Would he send over another? Spying the challenge in his silent gaze, she sat, drank the wine and rose again.

Another appeared, just as she'd expected.

"I really couldn't," she insisted, but the waiter wouldn't take no for an answer and she was left with a glass of expensive wine on the table in front of her.

Again the look in the mirror.

Great.

Though a part of her brain nagged at her that she was making an incredible, irreversible mistake, she felt bolder than she should have. Picking up the stemmed glass and carrying it carefully, she wove between the dancing couples and made her way to the bar.

"I suppose I should thank you for the drink—no, drinks," she said, unable to hide a trace of sarcasm in her voice.

"My pleasure." A crooked grin slashed across his jaw.

Damn the man but he was enjoying this. The twinkle in those blue eyes gave him away.

"Have a seat." He patted the vacant stool next to his.

She knew she shouldn't, but found it impossible to resist. "Trent Remmington," he said. To her horror she found his boyish grin incredibly endearing.

"Uh, Celia…" she said. Though tipsy, she realized

she couldn't admit her real name or true calling. Besides, she was just thanking the man for buying her a glass of wine. "Celia O'Hara."

"In town for the weekend?"

"Yes."

"Business or pleasure?"

"Just visiting my sister," she lied, telling herself she was getting into this way too deep. "You?"

"Convention here in town."

"Business, then?"

"For the most part."

"You live around here?"

"Houston, actually. As I said, just here for a convention." He finished his drink. "Want to dance?"

She hadn't danced in ages. "Dance?" She was certain she shouldn't. It wasn't a good idea to be this close to Trent Remmington when she was sober, let alone when she was feeling a little giddy. However the wine seemed to control her tongue and actions and she angled her head up and flirted outrageously.

"Why not?"

A million reasons raced through her head. This is dangerous. He's your client, for God's sake, whether he knows it or not. He's got a reputation for living on the edge. If he finds out you lied to him, it will be a disaster. A calamity! But she didn't stop herself.

The song was a slow country tune that she should have recognized but didn't. Trent's fingers touched her elbow, guiding her to the floor, and she felt her pulse leap. Oh, God, this was worse than she thought. He folded her into his arms and she realized she was in trouble. Big trouble. Kincaid-handsome, he was strong, smelled faintly of musk and he felt warm and, oh, so right. Her stupid heart began to race, and as his breath brushed her hair, she imagined kissing those blade-thin lips that she'd seen in so many of the photographs Larry had hidden away.

Of all the Kincaid heirs, Trent was the one who had touched her, who had reached through the reams of paper to find her heart. She felt as if she already knew him intimately, had shared his most private secrets, his quiet pain.

But that was crazy.

Or was it?

As the band's lead singer crooned an old love song, it seemed so natural to be held close to him and imagine she could hear the beat of his heart over the music, the buzz of conversation and the clink of flatware. Hundreds of tiny white lights winked through the boughs of the potted trees placed strategically around the patio and a soft, warm breeze caressed her face.

Though she wasn't the greatest dancer around, Trent made the steps seem easy. He held her close without crushing her, twirled her through the other couples without any effort, and never once did she even step on his toes. All in all, it was a miracle. A blessing. A…catastrophe! She couldn't be dancing with one of her clients, one who didn't even know he was the object of her search, one to whom she'd already lied.

When the song stopped, he held her a little too long and she could barely breathe. Her skin tingled and her heart was drumming in her ears. She wanted to sag against him, but fortunately he released her. She took one deep breath, then he took her hand and, after snagging their drinks from the bar, led her to a booth in a darkened corner where he settled onto a bench beside her. She tried to convince herself that she had to leave, that she couldn't trust herself this close to him.

"So tell me about yourself," he suggested, his thigh pressing against hers. Deep inside she started to melt. Swallowing hard, she picked up her glass and took a sip of wine that she suddenly wanted to gulp. "Are you married?"

"No." She held up the bare fingers of her left hand as proof and told herself that she was getting into hot water.

"Ever been?"

She shook her head.

"Why not? And don't give me some line about not meeting the right guy."

"Okay, I won't. I'm just a wallflower by nature."

His eyes narrowed on her and she had to swallow a smile. She'd worn a tight black minidress, strappy high heels, and added gold earrings and a necklace. She'd even gone so far as to twist her hair onto her head, letting only a few soft wisps fall around her nape and face.

"Wallflower," he repeated, then shook his head. "Nice try, Celia. But I'm not buying."

She lifted a shoulder. "You asked. How about you?"

"Been lucky so far. Never even gotten close."

She knew this, of course. He had a reputation of short-term relationships that never developed into anything serious.

"So are there any exes lurking in your past?"

"Not much of a past to lurk in, I'm afraid," she admitted, and he seemed skeptical.

"Got a job?"

"Paralegal. Thinking about becoming a lawyer." Jeez, how did these lies fly out of her mouth so quickly?

He cocked a dark eyebrow and took a sip from his drink.

She pretended she didn't know a thing about him. "So you're trying to convince me that you don't have an ex-wife and a dozen kids stashed away somewhere." Candlelight cast gold shadows across his bold features.

"No, I was lying earlier. I've really got four ex-wives and, get it right, fifteen children. Not just a dozen." He chuckled and his smile seemed more sincere, his interest obviously piqued.

Careful, Gina, you're treading in dangerous waters here, the sober, nose-to-the-grindstone private investigator part of her mind screamed. But the other part, the feminine, ludicrously romantic side, wanted to wade ever deeper and couldn't resist stepping closer to the whirlpool that she sensed was so near.

"So what do you do for a living that allows you to support all those kids and still leaves enough change left over to buy strange women glasses of expensive wine?" she asked innocently, wondering if he would tell the truth.

"Well, I'm a millionaire several times over, have oil wells and real-estate ventures all over the state, and saw you sitting all by yourself and thought you looked interesting."

She smiled and sipped her wine. "Does this line of yours usually work?"

"Usually." He said it without a trace of arrogance.

She wanted desperately to keep this game going, but she knew instinctively that she would only cause herself the kind of problems she didn't want or need in her life. She leaned over as if to kiss him, but said instead, "Well, it's not working with me. Not tonight."

"And you're a lousy liar."

"No, I—" With one hand he reached up and cupped the back of her head, and held her face firmly close to his. His eyes were suddenly so close she noticed the different shades of blue fusing together. His lips were near enough that when he spoke they brushed against hers.

"As I said, a lousy liar."

She gulped as she stared into those laser-bright orbs and tried to come up with some quick comeback. Was he going to kiss her? Oh, God, right here in the bar? With the dancers and the band and the other patrons? Pulse racing, she was suddenly and desperately out of breath. She licked her lips.

"Thought so," he said arrogantly. His hand dropped. So he'd been toying with her!

Like a frightened colt, she bolted. As she stood suddenly, her elbow hit her glass, splashing wine on Trent's shirt and suit, on his face, on the table.

"Oh, I'm—I'm sorry," she said, trying to swab up the spills and feeling her face turn as red as the wine. "Your suit..."

"It's all right."

She was mopping furiously with a napkin. "You've got to clean that before the stain sets. I'll pay the dry-cleaning bill."

"It's all right."

"No." She was insistent. "I mean, please, I feel like an idiot. The least I can do is pay for this." She motioned feebly to the red stain on his shirt and the drips still clinging to his jacket. "If you take it to the cleaner's you can send me the bill—" No, that wouldn't work. Even though she was a little tipsy, she knew she couldn't give out her real name or address; he'd catch her in her lie. "Or better yet, why don't you just give me the suit and I'll have it cleaned here at the hotel and get it to you tomorrow."

"Great idea. Let's go." He was on his feet in an instant. His fingers circled Gina's wrist as he dragged her with him. She wanted to argue, but when she started to protest, she saw the light of challenge in his eyes, the lift of one of his cocky eyebrows, the absolute belief that she wouldn't take him up on the offer.

"Lead the way," she said, fighting back all her rational instincts that told her she was not only flirting with the man but danger, as well. "If that's what you think we should do."

He sent her a glance that was pure sexual energy. "Oh, yeah. I do think." He said to the barkeep, "Put it on my tab." Then with Gina in tow, her head spinning from too much wine, he made his way to the elevator. Once in the car, he punched a button for the penthouse floor.

Her stomach knotted. What was she doing? Alone with him as the elevator sped to the top floor, she felt her feet beginning to chill. By the time the elevator car landed on the uppermost floor and the doors opened, Gina had a severe case of cold feet. "I'm not sure this is a good idea."

"I know it isn't." Still pulling her, he led her into a suite with a panoramic view of the city. The lights of Dallas blazed. Stars twinkled. Her head spun.

What am I doing here? she wondered, and nearly fell into one of two small leather couches angled around a glass-topped table that held a basket of fruit and an ice bucket with a bottle of chilling champagne. A gas fire hissed from a marble-faced fireplace and through double-glass doors she caught a glimpse of a king-size bed. Soft music played through hidden speakers.

Get out of here, Gina. Get out of here before you do something stupid!

"Pour yourself a drink. Anything you want." He motioned to a minibar tucked inside the wall unit as he walked into the bedroom.

"I think I've had enough. Done enough damage to your clothes."

"Suit yourself." He was already unbuttoning his shirt and rather than even be tempted to look at him, she walked to the windows and stared out at the city, where the traffic hummed and a few clouds dared venture across the moonlit night.

Just get out, Gina. As fast as you can! Take his clothes, send them down the cleaner's and then go back to your room and forget him. He's a client, or more precisely, the object of a client's quest. Don't forget it. It was crazy that she was anywhere near his hotel room, especially considering how she felt about him, the mental picture she'd drawn of him, the way she empathized with his rebellion and felt pride at what he'd accomplished on his own terms.

She had to leave and fast.

She heard him emerge from the bedroom and turned to find him in a clean pair of slacks and polo shirt. Barefoot. He strode to the table and without saying a word, opened the bottle of champagne and as it popped and foamed, poured two glasses. Carrying one in each hand, he walked to the bank of windows where she stood. She hoped she didn't look like a frightened doe caught in headlights.

Her pulse quickened with each of his steps and she forced her eyes away from the neckline of his shirt and the dark chest hairs springing from the open collar.

"Another bad idea," she said when he held out a long-stemmed glass.

"I guess I'm just chock-full of 'em."

"Appears so."

Reluctantly she accepted the glass. "How about a toast?" she suggested, intending to take one sip and bolt.

"You go first."

"Okay. How about, 'Here's mud in your eye'?"

A smile touched the edges of his mouth. "I expected something a little more original."

"Such as…?"

"To chance meetings." He touched the rim of his glass to hers and her heart did a silly little flip.

They both sipped and she managed to stare into his erotic blue eyes. "Or how about, 'To the art of dry cleaning'?"

"Why not?" Again he tapped his glass to hers. Again they sipped.

He didn't stop there. "Or to—let's see—how about 'To women who aren't always what they seem'?"

"Are you talking about me?" she asked, ignoring the increased tempo of her heartbeat.

"If the shoe fits…"

"Easy for a barefoot man to say," she teased, and he chuckled deep in his throat. "You don't know anything about me."

"Whose fault is that?"

"You wouldn't want to know."

One eyebrow elevated and the hint of a dimple creased his cheek. "Try me."

"I don't think so. Just trust me on this one." She was warm inside from the wine but feeling guilty for the lies she'd so glibly told him. But there was no way out of them now. That was the trouble with lies; one bred another and another and so on. She set her half-drunk glass on a side table where a vase of irises, birds of paradise and lilies overflowed. "I think I'd better leave. Where's the suit?"

"In the bedroom."

"Maybe you'd better bring it out."

She half expected him to invite her to go get it herself, but he nodded curtly and, leaving his glass beside hers, walked through the open doors again and returned with the black suit and shirt. "You don't have to do this," he admitted.

"Of course I do."

"It was an accident."

"I know, but I'd really feel better if you'd let me take care of it." She didn't want to argue, just make tracks.

"Why?" he asked. "Why would it make you feel better, since we both know you didn't mean anything by it."

"Accident or not, it was my fault." Oh, this argument was stupid.

He shook his head, tossed the suit onto a couch, cast a guilty glance at Gina and then out the window. "Maybe I should be honest with you."

Gina cringed inwardly at the words. "You haven't been?"

"Nope."

"You're not really a millionaire, is that it?" she said, though the joke fell flat and she already knew it was the truth.

"Nah, that's not what I was talking about." His blue eyes met hers with such an urgent honesty she nearly gasped. "I wanted an excuse to get you up here."

"Oh?" She swallowed hard.

"The dry cleaning was just a ploy. I don't give a damn about it."

"And once you got me up here?" she asked, sweating a bit, her heart knocking. Was it her imagination or had the temperature in the suite just gone up about fifteen degrees?

"I just wanted to get you alone."

Her heart began to jump now. "Why's that?" she asked, but she saw the passion in his gaze.

"Because, darlin', I think you're the most interesting woman I've seen in a long, long time."

"You…you don't even know me."

"But I'd like to." His expression was sincere, but she warned herself not to believe him.

"I bet you say that to all the girls who pour wine on your clothes."

His lips twitched. "You're right. All of them."

She felt an unlikely stab of disappointment.

"And all of them are right here."

"Imagine that. All the klutzes in one suite. Gee, Mr. Remmington, how did you manage that?"

"I'd like to say it was skill, but it was probably just dumb luck."

She giggled despite all her reservations. What was there about him she found so damned alluring? So sensual? Intriguing enough that she would cast down her natural defenses and throw all caution to the wind? She could rationalize from now until eternity, tell herself that it was because she "knew" him from everything she'd read and researched about the enigmatic bastard son of Larry Kincaid, but there was more to it than that. She was smitten with this stranger. Felt a bond with him he didn't even know existed. She was a fool, that was it. And she had to leave now.

As if he'd read her mind, he said, "You could stay."

Her heart nearly stopped. She was tempted, but no, she couldn't.

"I don't spend the night with strangers."

"You could get to know me first."

"I think, Mr. Remmington—"

"Trent."

"Okay. I think, Trent, it would take more than a couple of hours to get to know you."

"I can be very charming."

"Oh, please. Good night."

To her surprise and chagrin he didn't try to stop her. He lifted a shoulder. "Whatever you think's best, Celia."

That name again. Reminding her of her duplicity. "Just don't tell me I'm missing out on the opportunity of a lifetime," she said, scooping up the soiled suit, shirt and tie.

"Wouldn't dream of it."

He didn't so much as take a step closer to her. Again that ridiculous stab of disappointment. "Well, thanks for the drink, the conversation, and the champagne. I'll see that these are delivered before you check out."

"Thanks."

Feeling suddenly silly, she started for the door, then crossed the room and stood in front of him. Still holding the bundle of clothes, she said, "It's been interesting."

"Amen."

Impulsively she kissed his cheek. "Good night." That was the mistake.

He grabbed her then. He wrapped his strong arms around her, dragged her close, slanted warm, possessive lips over hers and kissed her so hard she couldn't breathe, couldn't think, could only hear her own heart-beat thudding in her ears.

Gina felt dizzy. She dropped the suit on the floor. His hands splayed across her back as if he owned her. Her mouth opened and he groaned as the kiss deepened. Somewhere music was playing and the room seemed to shrink. He tasted of Scotch and champagne. Her knees went weak, her resistance fled, and before she knew what she was doing she was kissing him back, molding her body into the tight fit of his, her knees turning to jelly.

Don't do this, Gina. This is pure madness. Get out. Get out now. While you still can!

But the alarms in her head went unheeded. She wrapped her arms around his neck and heard him groan as he lifted her off her feet and carried her through the French doors to the bedroom.

He didn't ask.

She didn't protest.

They kissed and touched and she remembered hearing the hiss of her zipper as it slid down her back, feeling a cool breath of air against her bare skin, discovering the wonder and strength of his body as her fingers explored the ridges and planes of hard, sinewy muscles.

She knew she was making an irreversible error, but she didn't care. She'd always been so cautious when it came to men, but this time, for this one night, she flung her reserve and distrust aside. She knew him, she rationalized as he kissed the crook of her neck and she began to ache inside. Strong, calloused fingers slipped her dress down her body and his mouth and tongue followed, his hot lips brushing her breasts, his warm breath blowing against her abdomen as he slid the silky fabric quickly off her body.

She sighed as every nerve in her body tingled expectantly.

She felt the corded strength of hard muscles pressing against her; reveled in the feel of her fingers playing in the soft matt of hair on his chest; kissed anxious lips that couldn't seem to get enough of her. Through the panes of the French doors, firelight sparkled.

She heard him kick off his pants, felt the strong muscles of his legs against her own, and experienced a wanting heretofore unknown to her. He breathed against her ear, the soft whisper of air tingling her ear, and as his fingers dipped past the lace of her bra, she wanted more. Everything. To discover what it was to be a woman—fully loved, if only for one night.

Closing her eyes, she moaned softly as his tongue and lips caressed her, seeking out each dimple in her skin. His hand parted her legs. She ached inside. Her back arched and she clung to him, her fingers digging into his shoulders. He touched her intimately, expertly, finding a place that stopped her breath.

Heat sang through her bloodstream and she'd never in her life felt such fever. She'd never known such want, such hunger.

By instinct she moved beneath him, swallowing against desire, needing the feel of him within her.

Hot. She was hot. Dots of perspiration broke out on her skin as he stoked heat in the most intimate part of her. She was clinging to him, gasping, opening. Desire thundered through her veins, throbbed in her brain. The room seemed to spin, or was it her soul? "Trent," she whispered, her voice hoarse, unrecognizable.

"Right here, darlin'."

"I—I want…"

"I know."

Desire pounded through her brain. She moaned—or was it his low, raspy voice she heard? He shifted, slid upon her and, kissing her hard, thrust deep inside her.

She gasped as she felt a jab of hot pain. But as he began to move, pain quickly became pleasure. He was everywhere at once, moving within her, kissing her neck, her eyelids, her lips, his hands caressing her as her mind spun out of control and the center of the universe existed in the spot that fused them together.

Faster. Harder. Hotter. She couldn't breathe, couldn't swallow, caught his rhythm, moving furiously with him. A billion stars flashed behind her eyes. Her mind spun with wild, erotic images and she cried out as the world seemed to shatter into brilliant shards of light. Body and mind convulsed.

He threw back his head and with a primal cry spilled into her, releasing himself. Letting go. He fell against her and sighed, his fingers twining in her hair as he kissed her cheek. "Celia."

The alias hung in the air.

Her lie.

Her deception.

She opened her mouth, determined to set the record straight. He kissed her again and all her good intentions fled. For this night, she would give in to the desperate urges of her body and when it was over, she'd leave. He'd never know the truth....

Until now, she thought as she stared at the broad expanse of Montana sky. High above, the moon gilded the Kincaid ranch with its pearlescent light. Somewhere far off a coyote cried and Gina rubbed her arms. How could she ever explain what happened? To Trent? To herself?

Was it possible?

"What's going on?" a deep male voice asked, and she visibly jumped.

Whirling around, she found herself face-to-face with Trent Remmington. Moon glow cast his face in silvery shadows and yet she was able to read his harsh expression and knew that whatever he had to say, it wasn't going to be pleasant.

"Nothing. I—I just couldn't sleep. Thought maybe some fresh air would help."

"Did it?"

"Not so far."

"I couldn't get any shut-eye, either," he admitted as he walked to the fence and leaned against it. "I kept thinking about the night we met in Dallas and how you lied to me."

Here it comes, she thought, expecting him to lambaste her for keeping her identity a secret. Instead, he blindsided her.

"I didn't realize it until the next morning," he admitted, obviously irritated with himself. "But that night we were together, it was your first time, wasn't it?" He sounded disgusted. With himself? Or her?

"I don't understand…" She let the sentence drift into the shadows.

"Sure you do. You'd never been with a man before, had you?" His lips compressed. "You—Celia, or Gina, or whoever-the-hell you are—were a virgin."

Five

"Excuse me," she said, and even in the moonlight he saw the blush staining her cheeks.

"You neglected to tell me you were a virgin."

"You didn't bother asking."

She met his gaze boldly, almost daring him to make some inane comment about being over twenty-five and saving herself. For what? Him? He doubted it and felt like a heel.

"Did it matter?"

"To me?" He shook his head. "But I thought it might to you." She lifted a shoulder beneath the white terry-cloth of that short little robe thing in what he considered measured nonchalance. Any woman who'd held off that long didn't take going to bed with a man lightly. And yet she was the one who had disappeared before dawn.

"It's not that big of a deal."

"What about Jack?"

"What?"

"The guy you were talking to on the phone. What about him?"

She snorted. "My sex life isn't any of his business."

He digested this, listened to the sounds of the night—a horse snorting in a nearby field, frogs and crickets competing for air space while a bat swooped from a hidden roost. "So what's your relationship with him?"

"If you want to know the truth…"

"Well, that would be a nice change of pace."

Her lips flattened together for a heartbeat, then she added, "Jack and I are very close. Extremely. He would understand. Now, if you'll excuse me, I think I'd better try and get some sleep." She started to march away, but he was tired of her flouncing exits.

"No way, lady," he said, grabbing hold of her wrist, spinning her back to face him and feeling how small the bones were beneath his fingers. "I think I deserve some answers."

"Why?"

"Because the ones I got in Dallas weren't exactly on the up-and-up."

"Maybe you just asked all the wrong questions," she fired back and jerked her arm away from him. He watched as she huffed off toward the house in a blaze

of self-righteous and, as far as he was concerned, unde-
served indignation.

"Women." He wanted to dismiss her, but somehow
she'd gotten under his skin. She had from the instant
he'd seen her sitting across the dance floor, alone, at a
table, sipping wine and dressed to kill. At first he'd
assumed she was waiting for someone. A knockout
redhead like Gina wasn't likely unattached, but when
the date he'd thought she was waiting for didn't show
up, he'd taken a chance and sent over a drink.

The rest, as they say, was history. He'd helped her
"spill" her drink, had plotted to get her up to his room,
but sensed that she wasn't comfortable, wasn't used to
one-night stands. Hell, neither was he. Not any longer.
But from his initial glimpse of her he'd known she would
be different. Interesting. Intriguing. And she hadn't dis-
appointed. Just thinking of their night together made him
hard. He'd woken up and found her gone, which was
unusual. No note, no trace of her. He'd called the front
desk and gotten no information on Celia O'Hara.

She'd just disappeared.

He'd decided to track her down, and felt like a fool.
Never in his life had a woman walked out on him. Never.
And he hadn't liked the feeling. So he'd gone so far as
to call a private investigator who'd done identity checks
on people he was considering hiring for Black Gold.
The man had come up empty. Celia O'Hara, the paralegal from Southern California, had disappeared.

Or, as he learned later, had never existed. Then out

of the blue he'd gotten that life-altering call from Garrett Kincaid telling him he wasn't Harold Remmington's son, after all. Hell, no, he was Larry Kincaid's bastard.

He'd been about to shelve looking for the woman, had even called his own private investigator and told him to quit searching—and now she'd fallen into his lap. Not as Celia O'Hara, the paralegal intent on becoming a lawyer, but Gina Henderson, a P.I. who had pulled the wool over his eyes and been investigating him, for crying out loud!

He kicked at a rock and sent it careening into a fence post. From the porch the old pooch gave up a soft woof.

The worst part of it was, he was still attracted to her. She'd lied to him, deceived him, played him for one helluva fool, yet Trent could hardly be around her without getting an erection that just wouldn't quit. It was ridiculous. Foolish. His reaction to her was way out of line, as if he were a horny nineteen-year-old kid instead of thirty-two and supposedly an adult.

But then everything about his life was a little out of whack right now. He'd considered phoning Blake and talking over the entire situation with him, but had decided against it. He and his twin, though identical in looks, were worlds apart in their thinking. Trent had always wondered about those twins who grew up wearing the same clothes, being each other's best friend, riding matching bikes. He couldn't imagine it. He'd been into leather jackets, jeans and T-shirts in high school. Blake had gone for a preppier look. Trent had ridden a motorcycle hell-bent-for-leather whenever he could, picked up more than his share of speeding tickets and was lucky he'd never spent a night in jail. Blake had driven their mother's car when they lived at home, a dependable sedan when they were away at boarding school, put his nose firmly to the grindstone and with the idea of becoming a doctor chiseled into his brain from a young age, had put his goal in front of everything else. He'd even married well, a girl from a socially acceptable family, then moved to California where he'd set up practice as a pediatrician.

Trent had almost envied his brother's vision for his life, but that vision seemed to be blurring as Blake had divorced and, if Trent had read the last telephone conversation correctly, Blake was looking for more in his life.

Whatever the hell that meant.

With a final glance at the stars, Trent slapped the top rail of the fence and walked toward the house. The smell of fresh-mown hay lingered in the air but was laced with the trace of Celia—damn, he had to get it right—Gina's perfume. If he listened real hard, he was certain he heard the rush of water through the creek that cut through some of the pastures. Horses nickered softly, grass rustled and the wind sighed through the few sparse trees. The old Kincaid house rose out of the land and sprawled wide.

Home?

Trent snorted and examined the mansion with a jaundiced eye.

He didn't think so.

* * *

"Okay, so where are we?" Jack asked from their office in L.A. as Gina, sipping coffee and fighting a headache from too little sleep, wedged the phone between her shoulder and ear. She was sitting in a worn leather desk chair in the den and was looking through the open window to a view of the stables and several interlocking paddocks.

"Garrett's talked all of the brothers into coming here. They start arriving early next week. Well, except for Trent Remmington. He kind of jumped the gun and showed up before I got here." Leaning back in the chair, she watched Trent and Garrett talking to Rand Harding, the ranch foreman. They were seemingly discussing the small herd of cattle that had just been driven into one of the pens, dusty coats catching rays of early morning light. Disgruntled, they bawled as the men who, deep in conversation, pointed from one steer to another.

"Gina?" Jack's voice brought her back to the present. "So, all of Larry's sons will be there?"

"Just the illegitimate ones, I think. Garrett didn't say a word about Collin or Melanie, the kids Larry had with his wife. So we're expecting six, five more. I still haven't located the baby or his mother." She frowned as this little mystery was the only part she hadn't been able to figure out. Who was the last woman Larry had been involved with and where was she? Gina had always relied on gut instinct and feminine intuition. Right now she had a feeling that Larry's youngest child, who was little more than a baby, was nearby.

"If the baby exists." Jack was skeptical. One note in a personal journal didn't mean that there was a seventh illegitimate son, or so he'd said time and time again. "Six is enough, don't you think?"

"I know, but searching through Larry's things, it just seems that there might be a much younger sibling." She took another swig from her now-cold coffee and frowned. "One who was born in the last couple of years."

"You're sure about this?" her brother asked, and her nerves were instantly strung tight. Jack was well-meaning but overprotective. He was often second-guessing her and always cautious, to the point that she wanted to scream. Eight years her senior and having spent time working for the Los Angeles Police Department, he was forever afraid she might get hurt.

"I'm not sure about anything," she admitted, blowing her bangs out of her eyes. "But I have this gut feeling that there's another son."

"Here we go again. Instinct over facts." He laughed and she imagined his hazel eyes crinkling in amusement.

"It's worked before."

"Can't argue with that."

"But you'd like to."

"Ah, baby sister, you know me well," he teased.

"Unfortunately," she cracked.

"So, how're you going to go about locating the kid?"

Gina's eyes narrowed as she thought. "I've gone through the regular channels, checked hospital records, birth announcements in the paper, adoption agencies and lawyers, so now I'm going to listen to some good old-fashioned gossip. There's a place where everyone in Whitehorn seems to gather—a diner called the Hip Hop Café."

"So what if that tack doesn't work?"

"Well, I don't know. Back to square one. I guess I'll just have to talk to Winona Cobbs, she's something of a psychic around these parts, I hear. Maybe she can just read some tea leaves or gaze into a crystal ball or read a few palms or something."

"Oh, brother."

"No, in this case, it's 'Oh, half brothers.'"

"Very funny," he drawled, then chuckled. "Listen, take care of yourself and—"

"Don't do anything dangerous. Watch your back and call you if there's a hint of trouble. Have I got it down, Jack?" She couldn't help needling him.

"I guess. Hey, one more question. How're you getting along with Remmington?"

She glanced back to the window and discovered Trent was no longer with Garrett and Rand. "That's a tough one," she admitted, "considering the circumstances."

"Well, keep me posted."

"Will do."

"Love ya, kiddo."

"Love ya, too, old man," she teased and, as she hung up, glanced at the date on the display of her laptop computer. It had been more than a month since the night she'd spent in Dallas with Trent and… Oh, Lord. A familiar worry wormed through her brain again. Her throat tightened as she stared at the date, then brought up the screen for April. There it was, big as life—the little mark she always made that reminded her of her last period.

More than six weeks ago.

Her heart sank.

She'd never been this late. Never.

Nor have you ever slept with anyone before…and unprotected sex at that. Oh, Gina, what were you thinking? You're smarter than this.

There had to be some mistake. Had to.

So she either was sick or she was pregnant.

It was time to find out which.

Winona prided herself on her ability to read people. It wasn't just their expression or their body language that gave away their inner thoughts. Oh, no. It was much more. She was certain each person's aura manifested itself, and if most people took the time, they, too, might view what she found so obvious.

As she walked down the dusty street, she noticed more than most people. Jordan Baxter had paused in the awning of the bank building, checked the lazy flow of traffic, then jaywalked across the street. He was concentrating so hard, his eyebrows cinched together under the brim of his hat, his lips all drawn up as if he'd been sucking on lemons. Anyone who glanced in his direction could tell that he was as mad as a nest of hornets just shot with a hose.

But Winona knew there was more to it than simple ire.

The look on Jordan's face was reserved for those times when he had to deal with the Kincaids. He'd never gotten over the fact that his mother had been just another notch on Jeremiah Kincaid's belt. Poor Jordan, he was forever trying to prove himself as good as the Kincaids. No doubt he'd heard a whole passel of them were due to arrive.

Jordan blew past and didn't even shoot his disdainful once-over her way. But then, he was a little intimidated these days. He'd tried to buy her land on the highway, attempted to force her out of the Stop-n-Swap, but she'd told him to leave her alone, that she'd ricochet all his bad energy back in his direction if he tried it. He'd laughed at her until a few little "accidents" had occurred all around him. Unnerved, he'd taken her advice to heart, backed off, and seemed to now save his frustrations for the Kincaids.

Well, good luck. In Winona's opinion, bad karma begat only bad karma. As long as Jordan dwelled on the negative, he'd never prosper. All his money and possessions would give him little joy.

She wiped at her head with a handkerchief and paused on her way to the bank when she noticed a rig pull into a parking spot in front of the Hip Hop Café. A tall redhead practically flew out of the shiny Ford. She was a pretty girl with a strong stride, determined set to her chin, and a no-nonsense attitude that caught Winona's eye. But there was more to her than that, Winona thought. This gal looked like a woman on a mission.

That was the trouble with the young people today;

they were all moving way too fast. The young woman, whoever she was, had better slow down because if she didn't she was headed for a fall. Winona had a sixth sense about these things.

"Oh, that Larry Kincaid, he loved women. Didn't matter if they were married or not. He charmed the socks off 'em. Well, the socks and a whole lot more." Seated at the first booth of the Hip Hop Café, Lily Mae gave an exaggerated wink, showing off an eyelid covered in bright blue eyeshadow.

"I'm tellin' ya, Gina, if there was a female within fifty miles of him, she was fair game as far as he was concerned," the little old lady said with a smug I've-seen-it-all smile. A friendly thing, Lily Mae was anxious to give out as much information as she could, but even she couldn't keep up with Larry Kincaid's exploits.

From her side of the both, Gina nodded and noticed that she was the object of more than one curious glance. "I'm talking about a woman he might have been seeing a couple of years ago, or a year ago, not long before he died."

"I'm thinkin', I'm thinkin'." Lily Mae swirled her iced tea and a slice of lemon pirouetted through the cubes.

"There were so many, it's pretty hard to keep them straight." Lily Mae glanced around the crowded café, always on the alert for the makings of more gossip. "Haven't you found a passel of his sons, already? All of 'em have different mothers, don't they?"

"Just about." Aside from Trent and his twin brother

Blake, the other four men had been brought into the world by different women. Gina tapped her fingers anxiously on the edge of the table until she realized Lily Mae was taking note of her case of nerves.

"Somethin' botherin' you?"

Only that I slept with the grandson of my client. That I lied to him and now have to face him every day, and that I might just be pregnant with his child. Other than that, things are just peachy. "I'm just trying to wrap this up," Gina said. That much was true.

As the waitress passed by, Lily Mae held up her half-full glass. "How 'bout a refill, Janie?"

Janie managed a patient smile as she quickly jotted an order from a nearby table onto her pad. "Coming right up," she said to either the two men from the sheriff's department who were seated at the next booth—or to Lily Mae, Gina couldn't tell which. The café was crowded, Janie nearly running herself ragged as she breezed from one table to another.

"They need another waitress here," Lily Mae mumbled. "Janie can't do it all herself."

"I think they're looking for one." Gina nodded to the Help Wanted placard taped to the inside of a window.

"Well, it better be soon."

"So, tell me about the women in Larry Kincaid's life."

"That would take forever. Oh, thank you dear." Lily Mae smiled brightly as Janie came by with a pitcher of iced tea. "Can I get you anything else?" she asked. "We've got fresh strawberry-rhubarb pie today."

"Oh, I shouldn't…" Lily Mae said, then lifted a shoulder, "but I can't resist. Bring me a piece with some ice cream. Vanilla."

"Anything for you?" Janie asked Gina as the ceiling fans slowly turned overhead.

"No, thanks."

"Oh, come on," Lily Mae insisted. "People come from miles around for the pies and donuts here."

"Fine," Gina agreed, more to be amiable than from hunger. "The same."

"You won't regret it." Lily Mae winked again as Janie refilled her glass then hurried off. "Now, as for the women in Larry Kincaid's life, let's see…" Lily Mae wriggled her fingers and started rambling on, her version of Larry's colorful life a mixture of fact and fiction. She paused only when the two slices of pie were delivered.

Gina was amazed and took mental notes of anything that seemed the least bit true.

"You know a lot about Larry Kincaid," she said.

"Well, that's true. I make it my business to know." Guileless, the older woman waved her fork at Gina. "Whitehorn's a small town. I just keep my eyes and ears open."

"So, who was the last woman Larry was involved with?"

Lily Mae was cutting off another bite from her wedge of pie. She stopped and thought for a second, little lines furrowing between her eyebrows. "You know, I don't really recall." Then, as if she'd let herself down, she shook her head. "I'll have to do some checking around."

So will I, Gina thought. *And I'm going to do it quickly.* The sooner she could get out of Dodge—er, Whitehorn, and away from Trent Remmington, the better!

"So, tell me about Gina," Trent suggested as Garrett surveyed the progress on the indoor arena that he'd ordered built as he hoped to train horses during the harsh winter months ahead. The framework was finished, the roof in place and the siding started. Frowning, pulling on a two-by-four to test its strength, he seemed satisfied that he was getting his money's worth from the construction crew he'd hired to update the paddock and repair the ranch house.

"What is it you want to know?" From beneath the brim of his hat, he slid his grandson a glance.

"You hired her to find Larry's sons." He just couldn't make himself call the son of a bitch who'd sired him "father." No way.

"Yes."

"And she did."

Garrett straightened, swatted at a horsefly, then rubbed his thumb over the head of a nail that had been driven into one of the two-by-fours. "That's about the size of it. Actually, I hired her brother."

"Brother?"

"Jack. He's really the owner of the private investigation firm. Gina works for him."

Trent's jaw slid to one side. So much for her mysterious relationship with Jack. He should have figured she'd lie to him again. "Does she?" he asked, and didn't bother hiding the sarcasm in his voice. He couldn't wait to confront her with this little bit of knowledge. He'd heard her talking to Jack on the phone yesterday morning and jealousy, ridiculous as it was, had burned in Trent's gut. He couldn't help himself. Where she was concerned, he was fast becoming a fool.

Garrett's gaze narrowed on his grandson. The grooves around the corners of his eyes deepened. "Well, there's more to it than that, I'd say. They're almost partners. Jack worked for the L.A.P.D. for years and he takes the more dangerous cases, mainly because he's protective of his little sis. But she's no slacker. I have the feeling she'd like more dangerous assignments, but she's gifted at what she does. She's developed quite a reputation for finding lost family members." He shoved the brim of his hat up with a thumb. "Found you pretty quick, now, didn't she?"

"I suppose."

"And that bothers you."

"Nope."

"Then maybe it's the woman herself that bothers you." It wasn't a question. The old man was pretty intuitive, Trent would give him that. "And I don't blame you. She's one good-looking, smart lady."

And a liar, Trent silently added. He wondered if he could believe anything that passed between those perfect white teeth. "I'm not in the market."

"How do you know?"

"I know."

Garrett didn't respond, just patted one of the posts and turned toward the house.

"Tell me about Larry. What's up with all these illegitimate sons?"

All amusement died in the older man's eyes and Trent, though he'd been loath to bring up a sore subject, felt he deserved the truth.

"I wish I knew." The old man sighed as they passed a corral where horses grazed in the late afternoon sun. "I sometimes think it might have been my fault, you know."

"How?"

"Oh, well…" Garrett's mouth twisted into an ironic smile. "Larry's mom was pregnant with him when we got married. I wonder if Larry thought, once he was old enough to do the math, that it was his license to promiscuity."

Trent snorted. The more he learned of the man who had sired him, the less he liked him. Whereas Garrett seemed to stand for truth, justice, the American way and everything good in this part of Montana, Larry had been just the opposite. "Probably he was just a bad apple."

"We've had more than our share," Garrett admitted, then stopped short and watched the lowering sun for a few minutes. "You may as well know, there's a lot of good blood in the Kincaid family, and a fair amount of bad."

"The way it is in all families," Trent observed.

Garrett raised a skeptical graying eyebrow. "We'll see. When the rest get here."

Great, Trent thought with more than a trace of sarcasm as he reached into his pocket and withdrew his keys. Just damned great.

Six

So what had she learned? Gina asked herself as she urged the palomino mare up a dusty trail in the foothills.

Only that you can't get Trent Remmington out of your head.

"Fool," she muttered under her breath. She clucked to the horse, encouraging the little mare into a gentle lope as they crested one of the hills on the western portion of the Kincaid spread. She'd been at the ranch for three days and hadn't gotten any closer to finding Larry Kincaid's seventh child than she'd been when she'd left L.A.

But she had a feeling that she was getting closer. Just being near Whitehorn spurred her female intuition into overdrive. Her fingers gripped the reins a little harder. She'd already scoped out the town, met some of the locals, delved into local history. She began to understand, for the first time in her life, why people chose to settle down in a small community over the fast pace and excitement of the city.

Or was it because of Trent? She could hardly turn around without running into him. He was either at the desk in the den of the house, running his business via fax, modem and telephone or helping Garrett and the work crew with the chores. She'd heard him argue with an investor one minute, then watched as he'd tugged on work gloves to help repair a barbed-wire fence the next. He'd gotten his hands greasy helping Garrett fix an oil leak in the old tractor, helped Rand cull calves that needed to be immunized another day, and offered Suzanne a cup of coffee, insisting that she "take a load off" and sit with Gina and Garrett at breakfast just this morning.

The playboy millionaire was far more than met the eye, a man who wasn't afraid of work, women or much else.

And she was falling for him.

"You're a case," she derided herself. She was here to do a job. Period.

And what if you're pregnant?

She closed her eyes for a second. Yes, what? Her mind spun at the thought. Breathing deeply of the pine-scented air, she felt the mare tense. Gina's eyes flew open as a startled bird flew across the path in a whir of feathers. She watched as the pheasant took cover in a copse of long-needled branches. Rays of sunlight piercing the overhead canopy spackled the trail with splotches of sunlight and shifting shadows.

Gina clucked to her horse. She'd decided to take this ride to get some exercise, explore the ranch a little and work the knots out of her mind. But she was failing. And the tangles she'd been trying to loosen only seemed to become more stubborn and tight.

Ears pricked, the mare accelerated into a bone-jarring trot and Gina tried to put order to the facts on the case. She'd found six of Larry Kincaid's sons, true, and there was evidence that he'd had another. There were unsubstantiated rumors that Larry had had a fling with a woman who lived near Whitehorn, but no one seemed to know with whom or if the rumors were true. Who was the woman he'd been involved with? Where was the baby? Gina had checked the birth records at the closest hospitals, read birth notices in papers of small towns surrounding Whitehorn, surfed the Internet and had come up dry.

And you're supposed to be a specialist when it comes to finding people, her P.I.'s mind nagged at her.

She had hoped to wrap up this case and move on. And get away from Trent Remmington. "Yeah, yeah, I know," she admitted to herself. But she'd failed. Her back teeth gritted at the thought. Failing was a word she didn't want in her vocabulary.

The path veered sharply to the right. Spindly trees gave way to a grassy meadow where wildflowers bloomed in profusion, speckling the sea of tall grass with small purple and white blossoms. A late afternoon breeze caressed her face and caught in Gina's hair. Now *this* was the Montana she'd read about, the place of romantic fantasies and cowboy tales.

And of maverick oilmen? She frowned at the thought and quickly banished it.

Soon she'd be faced not only with Trent but the other five sons Larry Kincaid had hidden from the world—grown men she'd found. She wasn't looking forward to meeting them. She still thought it best to keep a professional distance from the objects of her search.

How would the half brothers react? Until just a few weeks ago none of them had realized they'd been sired by a ornery cuss of a man who hadn't bothered to be a part of their lives. Yep, Larry Kincaid had been a piece of work.

She doubted any of the men would be thrilled to meet her. She pulled hard on the reins near a creek that tumbled and splashed its way downhill. Hopping off the mare's back, she let the horse graze and took a seat on a large flat rock at a bend in the creek. From atop the sun-baked stone she gazed downward to the heart of the Kincaid ranch. The indoor arena, nearly complete, was by far the largest building, and in the distance, she made out the foreman's house. Cattle and horses grazing on the surrounding acres were small dots in the rolling fields.

Gina kicked off her boots, rolled up her jeans and let her feet dangle in the icy water. She sucked in her breath. "God, that's cold." It all seemed so peaceful. Serene. Uncomplicated. She watched a butterfly flutter amid the blooms of wildflowers along the creek bank. It was a lie. Serenity was only an illusion. She had only to think of Larry Kincaid and the mess he'd made of his life and all the lives around him. Seven illegitimate sons. And never a thought to them.

Again she considered Trent. What would she tell him if she was pregnant? "Don't even think like that," she warned herself. So she was late in her cycle. So what? She was stressed-out. Majorly so. That was it. As soon as she could she would buy a home pregnancy test and that would be the end of that.

Unless she was going to become a mother.

Oh, Lord. She felt a moment's elation before she reminded herself that a baby wasn't exactly the kind of blessing she was expecting right now. Babies came well after a person was married and secure in a relationship. Right? Pregnancies were planned, unless you were a person like Larry Kincaid. Frowning at the thought, she absently rubbed her abdomen, then caught the gesture and stopped. There was just no reason to borrow trouble.

She had a job to do here in Whitehorn and she planned to finish it as quickly as possible, then return to L.A., her apartment near the University of Southern California, where she still took an occasional night class, and the private investigation firm where she worked with her brother. Inwardly she cringed when she thought about Jack. He would be devastated if he had any inkling she thought she was pregnant.

"Stop it," she growled just as she heard the sound of

hoof beats. The mare's golden head lifted and she nickered. Gina glanced over her shoulder. Astride a roan gelding, Trent appeared.

Gina's throat caught at the sight of him, backdropped by the blaze of a setting sun. Scrambling to her feet, she used her hand as a visor and squinted up at him. "You know, Remmington, we've got to quit meeting like this," she said as much to break the ice as anything.

The hint of a smile twisted his lips. "My thoughts exactly." He slid from the saddle and advanced upon Gina. Her heart knocked wildly and she thought he was as purely male and sexual as men came. His hair was windblown, his jaw darkened by a day's growth of beard. In faded jeans, boots and a shirt that had seen better days, he seemed a part of this raw, rugged land, at odds with the smooth-talking, slick businessman she'd met in Dallas.

"How'd you find me?" she asked, ignoring the heat she saw in his blue eyes.

"Just my infinite tracking skills."

"Oh, right."

"I think…no, I'm sure I have some Native American blood running through my veins. Isn't that right? Or maybe in a past life I was a tracker."

"Give me a break."

He laughed and the sound was deep and true, rising above the babble of the creek. "Okay, so maybe Rand saw you riding this afternoon and pointed me in the right direction."

"That sounds more like it," she admitted, and found his slash of a smile as infectious as ever. Why was it she couldn't resist him?

"It didn't hurt that you took a main trail."

"So how do you know about it, and don't give me any of that B.S. about being a native guide, okay? I'm not buying it."

His grin slid from one side of his jaw to the other. "Well, now, you know, I'd like to take all the credit, but I think my old pal Chester—" he patted the stallion's neck "—wouldn't much approve."

"And the reason you followed me is?" she asked.

"I thought we needed to talk."

"Uh-oh. Look, if it's about me lying to you about who I was, I think I already apologized. I made a mistake."

"*We* made a mistake," he said.

She inwardly winced. He was right, of course. Falling into bed together was wrong. Too much wine, too little experience, and a curiosity about the sexiest man she'd ever met had been a lethal combination.

"There's no reason to rehash it to death." She felt her palms begin to sweat a little and she was rambling. "I don't know what to say. I'm sorry I lied, it won't happen again. We had some fun and— Oh!"

His arm snaked out, he grabbed her wrist and yanked her hard against him. "Don't."

"Don't what?" she asked, breathless with surprise.

"Don't fake all this nonchalance, okay? Don't act like it was just fun and games or a quick roll in the hay."

"But it was," she countered, refusing to be seduced by words she wanted to hear. She ignored the denial drumming in her head. "What it was, Trent, was a one-night stand."

"That was your choice."

She felt as if he'd slapped her. "Wait a minute, are you trying to say that you and I would have…what? Dated? Gotten involved? What?"

"You didn't stick around long enough to find out, did you?"

"I thought it was time to leave."

"Maybe I should have been consulted." His gaze bored down at her with such intensity she wanted to squirm away. But she held her ground and swallowed hard when she noticed how dangerously close his lips were to hers.

Don't think that way, Gina, that's what got you into trouble in the first place.

"I, uh, I thought it was best to leave things as they were."

"Because you lied about who you were."

"That was part of it, yes."

"But someone who waits until they're twenty-seven years old…" He paused and must have witnessed the flash of surprise in her eyes, because he nodded. "Oh, yeah, I know how old you are. I've done my own little investigation since Dallas. How does it feel to be the one under the microscope?"

She jerked back on her arm, but he wouldn't let go. He just kept driving his point home.

"Anyone who's a twenty-seven-year-old virgin doesn't fall into bed lightly."

Angling up her chin, she said, "So you're telling me that because I happened to end up in bed with you, it had to be because you were someone special, someone I'd saved myself for, someone—"

"Oh, hell!" He kissed her then. His arms surrounded her and dragged her tight against him. Before she could protest or start to struggle, his lips pressed urgently against hers. Anger fired through her bloodstream, outrage sang through her mind, but her wanton body wouldn't fight back, *wanted* to melt against him.

Desire, friend or foe, caused her to ache inside, brought an intense sexual awareness that caused a weakness in her knees and a hunger in the most primal depths of her.

Oh, but she wanted to make love to him, yearned to have his hard body driving deep into hers. White-hot images of making love to him flashed behind her eyes, branding her brain. She saw taut, bronzed skin, a washboard of abdominal muscles and a thick mat of chest hair stretched across raw bone and sinew. Her breathing was suddenly shallow, her heart jackhammering.

Don't do this, her mind warned. *Gina, for heaven's sake, think! You lost yourself to him once before, don't let it happen again.* And yet her free arm wrapped around his neck. Her fingers brushed the hair at his nape as his tongue pressed urgently against her teeth and she opened to him. Kissing him felt so right, and yet was oh, so wrong.

She closed her mind to that hideous voice in her head that was screaming she was about to make yet another, life-altering mistake.

He sighed into her mouth and she felt one of his hands splay against the curve of her spine, the tips of his fingers tantalizingly close to her buttocks. Oh, Trent let me love you, she thought wildly, though she hardly knew the man.

He lifted his head, twined strong fingers in her hair and forced her to look into his hot blue eyes. "You make me crazy."

She smiled despite herself. "And here I thought insanity was just one of your natural charms, that maybe it ran in the family. Now *I'm* the cause?"

"Yep." His lips twitched.

"I'm not buying it."

One of his dark eyebrows cocked. "Maybe I should convince you."

"Oh, and how do you propose to do that?" she asked, flirting outrageously, daring him.

"Want me to show you?"

No!

"Absolutely."

"You're asking for it, lady."

"Am I?"

"Oh, yeah." Again he kissed her. Again her blood heated fast. Again her heart raced. His lips were hot, hard, demanding. What was wrong with her? He devoured her mouth and she did the same, kissing, nipping, biting until she felt his weight drag them onto the carpet of new grass.

"You know, Remmington, this is a good way to get grass stains," she managed to say.

"Is it? Hmm. I can't think of a better one." His hands rubbed her shoulders as he kissed her neck and cheeks. She trembled inside. His breath was hot against her skin. In between presses of his warm lips against her flesh, he said, "But if you're really worried about it, maybe we should take this off." He was already bunching the hem of her T-shirt in his hands, yanking the fabric over her head, baring her skin to the cool kiss of spring air.

Stop this. Stop it now, her mind screamed, but the warnings were lost to her.

"Then it might be wise for you to do the same. I already wrecked one set of your clothes."

"The suit and shirt are fine."

"And the tie?"

One side of his mouth lifted as she started unfastening the buttons of his shirt. "It's history."

"I was afraid of that," she said, her fingers fumbling as she tried not to stare at his hard-muscled chest or the alluring thatch of dark hair that nearly covered it. Flat nipples peeked out of springy nearly black curls and it was all she could do not to kiss each one.

"As I said, this is insane," she whispered as he settled next to her and traced the lacy outline of her bra with one lazy finger. Her stomach did a slow, sensuous roll.

He leaned over and kissed the top of one breast and she watched the sunlight catch a few strands of red in his thick brown hair.

"Can't argue." His breath caused goose bumps to rise on her skin and the feeling was divine yet wantonly unholy. Her head was spinning, her body craved more.

"I mean… We should maybe go back to… Oh—" She half-closed her eyes as his tongue followed the path his finger had taken. Within the soft cup of her bra, her nipple hardened and ached.

He looked up, noticed the want in her eyes and kissed her again. With a deftness that only comes with practice, he unhooked the back strap and the lacy scrap of unwanted fabric was tossed aside.

He touched the tip of one nipple and watched in fascination as it puckered. "You are beautiful."

Blushing, she attempted to roll over to hide her nakedness, but as she turned, he pushed her back onto the grass and stared directly into her eyes. With a calloused thumb, he circled her nipple and she moaned with a desire she'd never known existed.

How she wanted to feel his naked body on hers. She imagined the length of him stretched out upon her, touching her, kissing her, his erection pressing hard as he made love to her as he had before. Deep inside she melted, and as he kissed her breast, his tongue caressing and tugging at her nipple, she moaned, her eager fingers digging into the muscles of his shoulders, her body arching in an insistent demand for more.

His lips found hers and her mind began to spin. As if from a distance she heard the stream gurgling and a woodpecker drilling into the bark of a tree.

He lay upon her, the fly of his jeans hard against hers. Heat roared through her. She held him fast. He began to move and rub against her, denim against denim, friction mounting.

Somewhere not too far off, over the drum of the woodpecker she heard hoof beats. The mare snorted. Trent stiffened and lifted his head. "I think we've got company."

She froze. "No."

"Yes."

"Terrific," she muttered, scrambling for her clothes and feeling every inch of her skin turn red.

Trent rolled to his feet and tossed her clothes to her. She stuffed her bra into the back pocket of her jeans and pulled on her T-shirt. She didn't have time to tuck in the hem. In an instant Garrett Kincaid, astride a painted stallion, rode out of the woods.

Gina was certain her face was the exact hue of her hair. The man wasn't an idiot. It wouldn't take him too long to figure out what had been going on as she stood barefoot, her hair mussed, her clothes wrinkled. Trent's shirt was on, but not buttoned, its shirttails flapping in the breeze.

The expression on Garrett's face said it all. He wasn't pleased. Hard lines surrounded his mouth as his eyes narrowed on his newfound grandson. "Thought I might find you up here," he said as he swung to the ground as easily as if he'd been forty years younger.

"You were looking for me?" Trent asked.

"Yeah. Rand said the two of you had headed up this way. You got a call from your secretary. Said it was real important. Talk of a strike."

"Hell."

"Thought you'd want to know."

"I do."

Garrett's harsh, uncompromising gaze swung in Gina's direction. "And Jack's been calling for you." If he noticed her disheveled state, which, unless he was blind he couldn't have missed, Garrett had the good manners not to mention it.

"Guess we'd better get back." Trent tucked the tails of his shirt into his waistband.

Garrett's jaw slid to one side. With a curt nod, he walked back to the paint and pulled himself up into the saddle. "Might not be a bad idea, all things considered." He kneed his horse and the rangy stallion took off.

Gina wanted to die. The last thing she needed was for Garrett to think she'd compromised her professionalism. "Well, that was certainly embarrassing," she said, dusting off the seat of her jeans and walking to her mare.

"Nah. He didn't think a thing of it."

"What makes you so sure?"

Trent snorted. "He's Larry's father, right? Garrett Kincaid's already seen it all."

But Gina wasn't convinced as she felt her breasts swing free beneath her T-shirt. It wasn't that she was a prude, not by any means, but she was bending her own rules of professional conduct a little too far for comfort.

The trouble was, she decided fatalistically as she mounted the mare, when it came to Trent Remmington, she didn't seem to have a brain in her fool head.

Seven

"So what's goin' on with you and Gina?" Garrett asked as Trent, seated at a battle-scarred desk in the den, finally hung up from a long conversation with his secretary. Garrett had walked in, taken a seat in a folding chair wedged into the corner and waited for Trent to finish his phone call. Renovations were going on in the main house and the sound of saws, hammers and men talking between themselves could be heard as they worked to update the old Kincaid homestead.

"Between me and Gina? Not a whole helluva lot," Trent hedged, not wanting to admit that from the moment he'd first seen her in the bar that night in Dallas, he'd wanted to go to bed with her.

"Don't kid a kidder." Garrett leaned forward, clasped

his hands together between his knees and favored Trent with an eagle-eyed stare that was becoming all too familiar. "I've got eyes, you know, and though you might find this hard to believe, I wasn't born yesterday."

"And you might find this hard to believe, but I'm a grown man, can make my own decisions and don't need anyone to tell me how to run my life."

"That's just exactly what Larry told me years ago," Garrett countered. He rubbed his hands together, pursed his lips and looked as if he had something more to say.

"What is it?" Trent asked, certain that he wouldn't like the answer.

"I just hope you don't turn out like him."

"Ha!" Trent barked out a laugh. "Like Larry? No way."

"You didn't know him."

"Sounds like that might have been a blessing."

Guilt shadowed Garrett's eyes and he stood, his knees popping as he walked to the window and gazed past the bunkhouse, stable, machine sheds and paddocks. But Trent guessed Garrett's eyesight wasn't focused on the vast acres of ranch land that swept up to the forested foothills. Nope. His grandfather—hell, that was still hard to swallow—was looking inward, to a time and space only he could see.

"Larry had more than his share of faults, I can't deny it," Garrett said as a skill saw screamed from another wing of the house, "but I loved him nonetheless. Yeah, he was a womanizer, a hard drinker and a gambler. He gave me more white hairs than any son should, but he wasn't all bad. At least, I can't believe he was."

"Or you won't."

Garrett lifted a shoulder and rubbed the back of his neck. "That's probably more like it. Anyway, just be careful. Gina's a nice girl."

"No, Garrett, she's a grown woman."

The older man turned on the well-worn heel of his boot and leveled a blistering blue glare at his grandson. "A *nice* grown woman. Now, listen, I'm offering you some sound advice here—"

"I don't remember asking for any," Trent interjected.

Garrett ignored him and barreled on. "Don't do anything stupid. That's all I have to say. Use your fool head and keep your pants zipped." With that, he left.

Trent, still seated at the desk and holding a pen, clicked it several times in frustration. His jaw was clenched so tight it ached, and for the first time in years he felt like a schoolboy who'd just been chastised by the principal. He hadn't liked it then, he didn't like it now. Probably because his own thoughts had taken the very same path.

He swivelled in the creaky chair and stared through the watery panes of glass. Outside, about to climb into his truck, Rand Harding had paused at Suzanne's appearance from the back of the house. One booted foot propped on the running board of his pickup, he leaned against the open door, as if he was about to climb behind the wheel. Suzanne stood in the shade of a live oak, holding their baby on one out-thrust hip. Smiling and laughing, she winked at her husband as he moved toward her. Trent couldn't hear their conversation but witnessed their expressions—amusement and deep-seated affection—so evident in the curves of their lips and sparkles in their eyes. The discussion was short and when it was finished, she leaned forward and he kissed her, hard. As if he meant it. Even though they were married. She blushed like a schoolgirl, the baby put up a wail, and Rand, his cowboy hat pushed back on his head, grinned widely, as if he was the bad boy in high school who'd just stolen a kiss from the prom queen.

Trent dragged his eyes away. He'd never been a romantic, never seriously considered settling down. Well, maybe once, when he'd thought a girlfriend had been pregnant. Beverly, a willowy blonde, had told him about the baby, then suddenly, the next week, informed him that it had all been a mistake.

He'd had conflicting emotions at the time. Beverly had been a stockbroker and was used to making her own decisions. Sophisticated and hardheaded, she'd been exciting and clever, but he'd never been in love with her. When she'd said she was carrying his child, Trent had felt an odd mixture of emotions: an elation he hadn't expected, a surprising sense of propriety and protection. He'd decided to be a part of the baby's life, either by marrying Beverly or by demanding joint custody, but he hadn't had the chance. Though she denied it vehemently, even laughing at his discomfiture, he suspected Beverly had either lied about being pregnant in the first place, to manipulate him, or had decided on her own to have an abortion. Either way, he'd ended the short-lived affair because he'd been certain she'd put her career above her child. In his scope of the world, that just didn't pan out.

Oh, sure, he'd heard a lot about quality time, about how a woman these days could have it all, but he didn't think there was enough of one person to go around when the demands of husband, kids, job and house were thrust upon her. He'd seen enough of that firsthand. His own mother, a career woman who hadn't had time for her twin sons, had convinced him that he never wanted to tie the knot—especially not with some woman already bound to her job.

So he'd had his share of flings and one-night stands. No strings attached. He'd been careful—except for the night with Gina. That night had been different on so many levels. Truth to tell, he was more than irritated that Gina—well, Celia at the time—had summoned the gall to slip away from him while he was sleeping in that hotel room in Dallas. Loving and leaving had usually been his M.O.

But then, she'd been different from the get-go. He'd seen her, wanted to seduce her, and managed to pull it off. That accomplished, he hadn't been satisfied. He wanted more. Now, it seemed, he couldn't get enough of her.

Frowning, he dropped the pen into a cup on the desk and slid one more glance at Rand and his wife. The foreman had taken his place behind the steering wheel, started the engine and had turned around, looking over his shoulder as he backed out. Suzanne, a wide smile across her face, waved and urged the baby to hold up his tiny fist and open and close his chubby fingers in a mimic of his mother's goodbye.

Trent felt a heretofore unknown clench around his heart, as if he were actually envious. God, he was a fool, and yet he continued to stare voyeuristically at the tight-knit little family.

Rand's truck disappeared in a cloud of dust, and Suzanne, usually serious from what Trent could discern, held little Joe up high in the air and twirled around, spinning them both. The baby threw back his head and mother and child laughed merrily, as if they hadn't a care in the world.

For the first time in his life, Trent wondered if any part of that homey little scenario would someday be his.

Jaw clamped tight in disgust at the turn of his ludi-crously maudlin thoughts, he snapped the blinds shut. He wasn't a Peeping Tom, for crying out loud, and he had no interest in the seductive illusion of the Norman Rockwellian picture of family life. He had no time for envy, not in this lifetime.

Marriage and kids and the whole ball of family wax was fine for Rand and Suzanne. Hell, it was fine for most people.

Just not him.

Ever.

Running down blind alleys. Barking up the wrong trees. Winding up at dead ends. Every one of those clichés proved true as Gina shut down her laptop and winced against a headache that was building behind her eyes. Positioned on her bed with a long phone cord connected to one of the three lines running into the house, she rotated her neck and hated the thought that she'd been defeated.

That baby was out there. Somewhere. She just had to find him. Ever since she'd ridden back to the heart of the ranch yesterday, she'd avoided Garrett and spent hours at the keyboard, searching the Internet, using every available source, hoping for some clue as to Larry's seventh illegitimate son.

There was another reason she'd holed up in her room, she admitted reluctantly. She'd needed time to pull herself together. How had she let herself fall victim to Trent's charms all over again? Hadn't she learned anything?

She turned her attention back to the problem at hand— that of finding the elusive Kincaid. So far she'd come up dry. Rubbing her temples, she turned to the small metal box lying open beside her on the bed. All she had was a notation in Larry's handwriting indicating there was a possibility of another baby—a boy, but nothing else. Just a supposition because the timing was right. Nowhere did he indicate the name of child or mother, not even the date of birth. Gina had looked through all of Larry's belongings, hoping for a letter, a birth announcement, a copy of the birth certificate…and she'd ended up empty-handed.

"It's impossible," she muttered under her breath, then caught herself. She had to find the baby.

So much for being an ace detective, she chided herself. Think, Gina, think! She flopped back onto the bed and closed her eyes, but instead of clearing her thoughts as she'd hoped, resting only muddled her head with images of Trent dressed in a killer suit in the Dallas hotel, in jeans and a T-shirt on the ranch, with nothing but a sheet draped over his naked body. "Oh, you're hopeless," she said out loud, and decided it was time to face Garrett again. She couldn't very well hide in her room forever.

Besides, she had some other business to attend to— a little matter of purchasing a pregnancy test. She was about to grab her purse and keys when she heard the sound of footsteps on the stairs. Within seconds Trent was standing in the door frame and her stupid heart jolted at the sight of him. Handsome, rugged, and sexy as all get-out.

"Something I can do for you?" she asked as he stepped into the room, which seemed to shrink.

"I just wondered how long you were planning to stay here at the ranch." His eyes were dark. Unreadable.

"I—I don't know. Does it matter?"

"Probably not."

"I hadn't planned to stick around, but I've got this problem," she admitted, climbing to her feet. "I don't like leaving a job undone. Until I can figure out if Larry had another child, I'll probably hang out here. Is that a problem?"

"Could be," he admitted, folding his arms across his

chest and frowning. "You and I…we got off on the wrong foot in Dallas."

Oh, Lord, where was this going? Her pulse began to pound. "Yes, I know, that was my fault—"

"Both our faults." His tone was sharp.

"I shouldn't have lied."

"No, but neither should I have," he admitted, and she noticed a tic throbbing near one eyebrow. "You weren't the only one who stretched the truth."

"No?"

His jaw slid to one side. "Nope. The fact is that from the moment you walked into the bar, I noticed you. Thought I'd like to meet you and…" He sighed through his nose. "Oh, hell, Gina," he said, his eyes drilling into hers. "From the second I laid eyes on you I had one thing on my mind."

"Which…was?" she asked, standing only a few feet from him and staring into the most erotic blue eyes she'd ever seen.

"That I wanted to go to bed with you."

She swallowed hard. "Well…"

"I don't think that's a surprise."

"Just that you're being so…forthright…I mean, usually people don't discuss this kind of thing."

"It doesn't usually happen." He took a step closer. "At least not to me."

His lips were thinned. Pursed. As if he were disgusted with himself. For a second she thought he would kiss her. For a second it was all she could think of, all she wanted.

"But you changed that, lady."

Part of her was flattered, the other scared to death.

"I would have done anything," he said, reaching forward, touching her arm with those warm strong fingers, "anything to get you up to my hotel room."

Heat crawled up her neck. Invaded her cheeks.

She started to say something, but he placed a finger to her lips. "And so we both deceived each other. I'm coming clean because I think we should start over. With a clean slate. No lies."

Oh, God, she wanted to fall through the floor.

Tell him, her mind nagged, *tell him you suspect you're pregnant! Now!* But the words wouldn't come to her lips. What if her worries were all just a false alarm, that her cycle was just messed up, that there was no baby?

"Deal?" he asked, so close his breath fanned her face. He dragged his finger down her lips and lower, over her chin and throat.

She could barely breathe. "D-deal," she repeated, and a hint of a smile touched his eyes.

"Fair enough." He hesitated a second, as if he was thinking about kissing her or pulling her close or tossing her onto the bed and making love to her, but he didn't. Instead he walked out the door and Gina was left with the fragments of another lie still hanging in the air. A much bigger lie.

There was a possibility that Trent Remmington was going to be a father. She leaned against the wall and bit her lip. If she chased after him now and breathlessly told

him her fears, she'd look like a foolish, desperate
woman. No, she had to wait.

Until she was certain herself.

Janie stared at the girl at table six. Seated all alone,
reading a paperback while she waited for her food, she
seemed out of place in the bustle of the dinner crowd.
Nearly every table was full and there was so much conversation that the music from the jukebox, some old
Patsy Cline song about heartbreak, was barely audible.
Cutlery and glassware clinked, conversation buzzed and
laughter rippled as the ceiling fans whirred overhead
and the deep-fat fryer sizzled in the kitchen.

The girl, all of twenty-two or twenty-three, Janie
guessed, was dressed in black slacks and a white blouse
with the sleeves rolled up. Thick glasses were propped
on the end of her nose, wavy red-brown hair was clipped
to the back of her head, and she wore little makeup.
Every few minutes she glanced up from the novel that
didn't seem to be holding her attention, then took a quick
look around the diner, as if she were sizing up the crowd.

Some of the Hip Hop regulars had shown up. Lily Mae
Wheeler, Winona Cobbs and Homer Gilmore, the old guy
with long gray hair and equally long beard who spent as
much time in the hills spotting aliens as he did in town,
had claimed their usual spots. Most of the patrons Janie
recognized and called by name, but a few strangers were
sprinkled about and more streamed in, filling up the
booths and tables faster than the busboy could clear them.

Janie breezed between the tables, took orders, brought drinks and food and tried to ignore the fact that her feet were beginning to ache from the long hours she'd put in this week.

The girl with the paperback absently chewed on the edge of her lip and every once in a while eyed the Help Wanted sign taped to the front window. "Order up," the cook yelled, and Janie scooped up four platters of steaming food. Balancing the plates carefully she wended her way through the tables to a booth in the corner. "Chicken-fried steak?"

"Right here," a cowboy with red hair, freckles and Western-cut shirt said. He was a regular who hired out as a ranch hand on several of the nearby spreads. As she set a couple of Reuben sandwiches and a Cobb salad in front of each of his friends, the cowboy used two fingers to motion Janie closer. His gaze was fastened on the girl at table six. "Don't suppose you know the gal over there with her nose stuffed into a book, do you?" he asked.

"No." Janie shook her head. "This is the first time she's been in."

His brow creased. "Think she's just visitin'?"

"I wouldn't know. Is there anything else I can get you?"

His friends shook their heads and dug into their food, but the cowboy was distracted.

"Order up!" A bell rang as the cook yelled just as the Patsy Cline tune ended.

"I guess I'll just have to find out," the cowboy said

as Janie hurried back to the counter to pick up an order of burgers and fries.

From the corner of her eye she noticed the cowboy saunter over to the bookworm's table. Grabbing the coffeepot, Janie headed to Winona Cobbs's table.

Winona was eyeing the girl with the paperback when Janie came to refill her coffee cup. "Who's that one?" Winona asked as she tore open a small package of cream. White clouds appeared in her cup as she drizzled in half the packet. She hitched her chin in the direction of the girl.

"You're the psychic," Janie teased. "You tell me."

"All right." Small lines appeared between Winona's graying eyebrows. "To tell you the truth, I think she looks like Lexine Baxter."

Janie nearly dropped the carafe of coffee. "Lexine? No way!" Lexine was pure evil and now in prison for crimes ranging from prostitution to murder. It was Lexine who had killed several of the Kincaid clan, including her husband Dugin and father-in-law Jeremiah. Janie shivered at the thought of the beautiful, seductive, and depraved woman. Thank God, she was locked away forever with no chance of parole.

"Yep." Fiddling with a crystal pendant that swung from a chain around her neck, Winona cast another look at the girl at table six.

Obviously embarrassed by the cowboy's attention, the newcomer blushed and swallowed, forced a smile she obviously didn't feel, and looked as if she wanted to drop right through the floor.

"Well, I'm talkin' about when Lexine was younger, before she had all that plastic surgery and she discovered that blondes really do have more fun." Winona narrowed her eyes. "Take off that one's glasses, dye her hair, and I'm tellin' ya, she's a dead ringer for Lexine."

Janie wouldn't believe it. She shuddered inwardly.

"You're way off on this one."

The door opened and more customers streamed in.

"Don't think so. There's Baxter blood in that one, unless I miss my guess, and there's something more. Look at the way she's trying to ignore the boy who wants to flirt with her. It's not natural."

The cowboy had placed a hand on the table and was leaning close, obviously interested, but he wasn't getting any kind of positive response. Finally giving up, he returned to his seat, grabbed his knife and fork and tore into his steak.

The poor girl stared at her book, but Janie noticed she didn't bother to turn a single page. Something was troubling her, and Janie knew the signs all too well. Worried glances, pursed lips, shadows darting through her eyes—all accompanied by heavy sighs. "You know, I'd bet that she's here in town to mend a broken heart. She could have just broken up with someone." Then, hearing herself, Janie shook her head as Elvis began to croon through the speakers. "Not that it's any of my business."

"I'm still saying she looks like Lexine in her younger days," Winona insisted, sipping from her cup. "I mean, without all that bad energy she conjured up later."

With a wave of her hand, Janie dismissed Winona's comments. Besides, she wasn't about to lump all the Baxters into one immoral pot. While Jordan had started out poor and made the best of a bad situation, returning to Whitehorn a prosperous, if not a kind man, his cousin Lexine had taken to a life of heinous crime. Though there was no doubt that both Lexine and Jordan hated the Kincaids, their need for revenge and the same grandparents were about all Jordan and Lexine had in common.

To think that the girl in the big glasses looked anything like the murderess was more than Janie could imagine.

"Take care of table eight," she told the busboy just as the bell over the door rang again and a group of teenagers swaggered in, laughing and joking, before sliding into a corner booth.

Sweat prickling her brow, Janie started for the table, but the girl who had been reading caught her attention as she was about to hurry past. "Excuse me." She looked up at Janie. "I don't mean to bother you, but I couldn't help but notice the sign in your window and I thought... I mean—"

"You want the job?"

"Yes. I'd like to fill out an application." Large hazel eyes gleamed behind pop-bottle-thick lenses.

"Do you have any experience?" Janie asked the younger woman.

"A little."

"Tell you what," Janie said. "Go grab an apron from

a cupboard by the back door. The cook will point you in the right direction. There's a pen and receipt book in the pocket. Then come back and start working." She gave the newcomer quick, basic instructions.

"I—I'm hired?" the girl asked incredulously.

"For tonight. Think of it as a trial run."

"Wow." She brightened, and Janie motioned to the busboy to clear her table.

"Just one more thing," Janie said as the girl started for the kitchen.

"What's that?"

"I'm Janie Austin. I'm the manager here. What's your name?"

"Emma. Emma Stover."

"Nice to meet you, Emma," Janie said with a smile as she wiped a droplet of sweat from her forehead with the back of her hand. "Welcome aboard."

"What do you mean, 'real friendly'?" Jack Henderson asked as he held the telephone receiver to his ear and paced in front of his desk. Glancing out the window, he spied cars whipping up and down the palm-lined street just a couple blocks off Sunset Boulevard. A thin layer of smog had Los Angeles in a choke hold, but that didn't stop roller-bladers and pedestrians from walking on the bright sidewalks.

"I mean, I saw Gina and Remmington dancing there in the hotel bar, oh, about five, maybe six weeks ago." Herb Atherton laughed, and the sound was nearly dirty.

Jack had never much liked Herb, whose credentials included a law degree but who did little in Jack's opinion to improve the legal system. Herb was and always would be a taker, a man who had the morals of an alley cat and yet had cultivated the ability to look down on others as if he were related to God. Herb didn't know the meaning of the word loyalty, but, if the price were high enough, he was willing to do whatever it took to win a case—right or wrong.

"Is that right?" Jack felt the vein above his eye begin to throb. Gina hadn't mentioned meeting Remmington. In fact, he'd thought she had planned to go to Montana, locate that last heir, if he really existed, then get out. She hadn't been interested in meeting Larry Kincaid's brood of illegitimate children, had even balked when Garrett had asked that she be present when they all arrived in Whitehorn.

"Yep, *real* friendly, if ya know what I mean."

Jack wanted to reach through the phone and strangle the smug attorney, but he somehow managed to hang on to his patience. "Gina didn't mention it."

"I'll bet she didn't. She spilled wine all over the guy, then gushed and apologized and ended up going up to his room—you know, to get the stains out or something." Another nasty laugh that ended in a coughing fit.

"Was there something you wanted?" Jack asked, trying to hide his irritation.

"Yeah, I need a little help trackin' down a dead-beat father," Herb said, suddenly very serious. "The jerk up and left the ex-wife and five kids high and dry about six months ago. I thought maybe you'd want to team up and help me out."

"That's really Gina's department," Jack said, the muscles tightening at the base of his skull whenever he heard about a man walking out on his family. Losers, every one of them—his own father included. "I'll have her give you a call when she gets into town."

"Do that." Herb hung up and Jack was left with a bad taste in his mouth. He didn't like Herb Atherton's insinuations about his kid sister, but then, Herb wasn't one to spout off without at least a seed of truth to back him up.

"Damn it all," Jack growled, wishing Gina would wind up the Kincaid case and hightail it back here. He was always a little restless when she was gone, though he knew he was being overprotective, just as he'd always been. Yet he couldn't help but feel responsible for her. He was the one who'd started the agency when he'd had it up to his eyeballs with the red tape of working for the L.A.P.D. Domestic violence, drugs and gangs had jaded him and at the first opportunity he'd quit the force and gone into business for himself.

Gina, after graduating from college, had begged to join him, and he'd reluctantly agreed to let her be a part of the team. He figured that at least he would be able to keep an eye on her. The kicker was that she'd proved herself to be one helluva investigator, especially when it came to tracking people down, and eventually Jack had made her his partner.

Until now she'd proved herself to be levelheaded, smart, efficient and professional.

So what was she doing with Trent Remmington?

He picked up his cup of now-cold coffee, walked over to a potted avocado plant and tossed the dregs into the soil.

When their old man had left, Gina had only been four years old. Jack, all of twelve at the time, had decided then and there that he'd take care of her. And he had.

Until now. Or so it seemed.

Swearing under his breath, he reached for his Lakers' cap and strode out the door. It slammed with a bang behind him and the heat of the city hit him full-force. Not that he cared. He'd go for a run along the beach at Santa Monica, think long and hard, then call his sister in Montana and ask her what in the hell was going on.

Eight

"Just tell me this, Gina, and give it to me straight. Are you involved with Trent Remmington?" Jack demanded from the other end of the line.

Gina's back muscles tightened as they always did when her brother pushed his way into her personal life. But, standing in the middle of the kitchen, she couldn't get into it with him now. She twisted the cord around her as she turned her back to the table where Garrett and Trent nursed cups of hot coffee and mopped thin pancakes through rivers of maple syrup. Suzanne, humming softly, was already stripping off her apron as the scents of bacon grease and java were blown around by a breeze rolling through the open windows.

"I don't see that it's any of your business," she said, keeping her voice low.

"Hold it. Stop it right there, Gina. We had a deal, you and me. We *don't* get involved with clients, or subjects of our searches or—"

"Murder victims?" she teased, trying to lighten the mood while silently praying that Trent wasn't listening. He and Garrett had been talking about Blake before the phone had jangled.

"Don't try to be cute, okay? I'm not in the mood," Jack growled.

She could envision the lines of disapproval bracketing his mouth. "And don't you blow a gasket. I know what I'm doing."

Her brother snorted and she wished she could reach through the phone lines and shake some sense into him.

"I am twenty-seven, you know."

"Old enough to avoid a mistake like this."

"Just trust me," she whispered. With any luck, her words were drowned out by the shouts of workers who had already arrived, intent on getting on with the job of renovating the place. Hammers pounded and a tractor started up outside, the rumble of its engine adding to the curtain of noise. "This is my life," she reminded her brother.

"Damn it all, Gina, you *are* involved!" He swore a blue streak before somehow managing to retrieve a bit of his composure. "You should know better."

"And you should butt out."

"Didn't you say that Trent Remmington is a rich playboy? A maverick oilman? A gambler?"

With each charge she cringed. If her brother only knew that she worried she might be pregnant. What would he say then? Well, he couldn't find out. He'd have a stroke, Garrett would go through the roof, and Trent would probably think she was using the baby to blackmail him into a relationship. Oh, Lord, what a mess. The hammering stopped and the tractor drove off, the sound of its engine fading. Again she lowered her voice. "I know what I'm doing, Jack," Gina lied, unconsciously crossing her fingers. "I would appreciate you having some faith in me."

"Holy Toledo." There was a moment's pause in the conversation, then he sighed loudly and she pictured him running stiff, frustrated fingers through his brown hair while his hazel eyes darkened with concern. The little scar on his chin, a result of a tango with a knife-wielding crack addict, was probably more pronounced as his anger rose.

"And, by the way, since when did you start listening to gossip?"

"Oh, give me a break, Gina."

"You give me one. Herb Atherton? Please!"

"Okay, so Atherton is slimy, I'll grant you that, and he'd sell his grandmother if he thought it would guarantee him a judgeship, but he usually gets his facts straight."

"The jerk should mind his own business. And so, brother, dear, should you."

"I am, Gina," Jack said, his voice tightening into the big-brother timbre she recognized and resented. "This is my agency and—"

"And I thought we were partners."

"We are but—"

"Then for God's sake, trust me, and don't come unglued. I'm handling everything, okay?"

She hesitated. Was it her imagination or had the kitchen become suddenly so still you could hear the proverbial pin drop?

She cleared her throat. "The rest of the half brothers are arriving in a few days, so if you're done, I think I've had my fill of browbeating for the rest of the day. But call back next week. I'll probably be under quota by then." She slammed the receiver back into its cradle. Turning, she found Garrett and Trent pretending to show interest in their clean plates while Suzanne, hanging her apron on a hook near the back door, lifted a curious eyebrow before saying, "I'll be back in a few hours." The screen door slapped shut behind her.

"Trouble?" Garrett asked as Gina settled into her chair where her breakfast of fried eggs, bacon and pancakes had congealed into a swamp of melted butter and syrup.

"Nah." She shook her head.

"I heard the browbeating comment," Trent remarked, and there was a tension near the corners of his mouth she'd never noticed before.

"Oh, it was just my brother. He can be a real pain sometimes."

Trent nodded but didn't seem convinced. He took a long swig from his cup. "I know about brothers."

"And you'll get to know more, real soon, unless I miss my guess," Garrett observed, rising to glance out the window as a sleek black Acura purred into the yard. "Looks like the first one's just rolling up now."

"Already?" Gina asked.

"Yep." Garrett's eyes narrowed as the man behind the steering wheel stepped out into the bright Montana sunlight. "Appears that twins are more alike than they might want to admit."

Gina moved to stand beside Garrett and braced herself. Trent scraped back his chair without so much as cracked smile.

The new arrival pulled a smooth leather suitcase from the backseat and when he straightened, Gina caught sight of his features for the first time. Straight brown hair, high cheekbones, thin lips—identical to those of the man striding to the back door to greet him.

Blake Remmington had arrived in Whitehorn.

"So I'm not the first," Blake said as Garrett and Trent strode across the parking lot.

Trent forced a smile he didn't really feel. He and Blake had never gotten along. He didn't expect their relationship to change just because they now knew that their mother had lied to them and that they were, in fact, Larry Kincaid's sons. True to form, Blake was dressed in tan slacks, an open-necked polo shirt, and polished loafers. No jeans and boots for this guy, Trent thought, not even in Montana.

Garrett stretched out his hand. "Garrett Kincaid. Your grandfather. It's probably easier if you just call me by my first name."

Trent noticed an entire gamut of emotions run across Blake's strong features as he took the old man's outstretched hand. "Glad to meet you."

"Same here."

Blake's gaze moved past Garrett to land full-force on his brother. "Trent. You're here early, aren't you?"

"Just couldn't stay away," Trent drawled, knowing he shouldn't bait his twin, but unable to stop himself. "What about you?"

"Once I got the phone call, I took care of business, threw some things in a bag and started driving."

"Pretty spontaneous for you," Trent observed.

"Yeah, well, maybe I've changed."

"Is that just after hell froze over?"

"Right before." Blake gave his brother an exaggerated wink. "Give it a rest, okay?"

"I'll try. No promises."

"Fair enough." Blake nodded curtly but not one of his perfectly combed strands of hair had dared fall out of place. Though more people than Trent wanted to admit had insisted that he and his brother were dead ringers, they didn't have a whole lot in common.

Unless, of course, you excepted that their mother had been a lying, social-climbing witch whose only concern was the advancement of her career and their father had been a womanizing cheat. They did have those terrific traits to share.

Trent winced inwardly at the thought of how much his night with Gina had mirrored his biological parents' meeting. Their mother had been a Montana state commissioner when she'd had the bad luck to run into Larry Kincaid at a Ranchers Association convention. After too many drinks and a roll in the hay, she'd found herself pregnant. Somehow, Barbara managed to convince Harold Remmington the boys were his and they'd married.

"Trent arrived a few days ago," Garrett explained casually.

Blake's blue eyes, so much like his own, found Trent's and, though the slight tensing of his brother's shoulders or the touch of disapproval in the curve of his lips was hardly noticeable, Trent saw it. He'd also bet that the old man hadn't missed a single strained nuance between the brothers.

"Trent was never known for his patience." Blake forced a handshake. It was strong, firm, and brief. "How've you been?"

"'Bout the same," Trent drawled. He'd never been one to confide in Blake. Oh, sure, whenever he'd gotten himself into a mess now and again, he'd had to turn to Blake, but that had been years ago.

"Still wildcatting?"

"Yep. What about you?"

"Well, things have changed a bit since Garrett called."

Trent heard footsteps behind him and Gina appeared. "Excuse me," she said, and stuck out her hand. "You must be Blake."

To Trent's irritation Blake's blue eyes sparked and his smile widened. "And you're…?"

"Gina Henderson," Trent said quickly before Garrett could make introductions. "Seems Gina was hired to track us down."

"Congratulations," Blake said so warmly and smoothly that Trent thought he might be sick. The guy was like warm pudding. Trent had forgotten how women had fallen at his brother's feet. Even now. Gina wasn't immune.

"Let me help you get your things," Garrett offered. "You can either stay up here in the main house or in the bunkhouse. Plenty of room in either."

"Doesn't matter where." Blake took a sweeping view of the place and as his gaze moved from the two-storied house to the stable, bunkhouse and outbuildings, he actually smiled, as if he liked the raw, rugged acres that unfolded in a patchwork of fields. "It's pretty up here."

Garrett practically beamed. "I think so."

"Bet you're not the only one," Blake said.

Garrett, rather than nod proudly, sobered. "No," he said, but didn't elaborate. "Let me help you with these."

Along with his suitcase, Blake had brought a brief-case, laptop computer and another smaller bag, all of the same matching leather, every piece engraved with his initials. Probably Blake's ex-wife Elaine's doing.

"Stayin' awhile?" Trent asked.

"I think so, yeah." Blake squinted against the morning sun as a warbler sang from a nearby tree and carpenters banged their hammers at the site of the new arena. "If that's all right with you," he said to the weathered man who claimed to be their grandfather.

"The longer, the better," Garrett said, grabbing Blake's laptop. "I think we all need to get to know each other."

"What about your job?" Trent asked. He'd never seen his brother so laid-back before. For as long as Trent could remember, Blake was always on a schedule, or a regimen. The son with a plan. As far as Trent knew, his twin had never faltered in his path.

"I'm taking a month off. At least. Maybe longer." They started toward the main house and Blake eyed the horizon. To the northwest the jagged snowcapped peaks of the Crazy Mountains loomed upward to a few hazy clouds. "Even doctors need some time off." He glanced at his brother. Deep lines creased his forehead. "Thing's haven't been great."

"I heard about the divorce."

Sadness touched his brother's eyes. "It wasn't meant to be, I guess. Elaine and I…" He shook his head and frowned. "Well, it's all water under the bridge now."

For the first time in a long while, Trent felt a pang of sorrow for his brother. Even though Trent could have told Blake way back when that social-climbing Elaine Sinclair wasn't the kind of woman who would want to stay home and raise the couple of kids his pediatrician brother longed for. Elaine had liked money, social events, and knowing who was doing what. She'd had visions for her doctor-husband and herself that didn't include her getting pregnant and fat or baking cookies or coaching soccer or attending dance recitals for a "snot-nosed brat." Why Blake hadn't seen it, Trent had never understood.

Blake had married Elaine and, upon her urging, taken a job in Southern California. Life in the fast lane of Los Angeles hadn't been Blake's cup of tea. Trent had known it from the get-go, but Blake hadn't asked his opinion at the time and Trent probably wouldn't have given it if he had. He figured each man made his own mistakes and paid for them.

At that thought, he glanced at Gina. God, she got to him. Even now, dressed in a pair of dark shorts and a pale yellow sleeveless blouse, she was sexier than any woman he'd met in a long time. Her hair turned to flame in the morning light and her little nose, spattered with those nearly invisible freckles, wrinkled when she laughed. Her smile was infectious and her legs, slim and tanned, seemed to go on forever.

Yep, he was hooked, he thought as he climbed the steps and held open the door.

And it ticked him off. Just as the spurt of jealousy he'd felt when she smiled at Blake bothered him. He'd never been the jealous type. If anything, he'd been the one who inspired jealousy and now that the tables were turned, he didn't much like the new feeling.

Once inside, Garrett led Blake up the stairs and offered him a room next to Gina's. Not that it mattered, Trent told himself as he set the bags he was carrying on the rag rug near a small bureau. Yet Trent's damned jaw hardened to the point it ached.

"Fixin' the place up?" Blake observed as two workmen carrying buckets of paint walked toward the back of the house.

"A bit. It was pretty rundown." Garrett placed Blake's laptop on his bed and glanced out the window. "Looks like Rand might need me," he said, spying the foreman striding toward the house. "Why don't you have Trent and Gina show you around? They've been here a few days." Garrett started to turn toward the door, but Blake grabbed him by the shoulder.

"Thanks, Garrett," he said, as if he were genuinely glad to meet the older man and embrace this chaos of a family. He threw out his hand again and clasped Garret's palm hard. "I'm really glad to be here."

"That's good to know, son." Garrett's smile touched his eyes. He clapped Blake on the shoulder. "Good to have you."

Trent strode out of the room. He couldn't stand another second of all this fake family togetherness over Larry Kincaid's bastard sons.

He'd never really gotten along with Blake and didn't think he'd fare any better with the rest of his half brothers. But then, he'd always been a loner. Finding out that Larry Kincaid had been his father hadn't changed things.

He left the room and hurried down the stairs to the den where he could bury himself in the faxes and e-mail that were streaming in. He heard Gina's laugh follow after him and he scowled to himself at the thought of her being amused by his brother.

Man, you've got it bad, he thought, jealousy sneaking through his veins again. And for a woman who lied to you, hopped into bed with you and then snuck away in the middle of the night. She played you for a fool.

Inside the den, he kicked the door shut and snagged up the receiver, intent on calling his secretary, lawyer, accountant, and an outside investor, but his fingers hesitated over the buttons and he listened for the sound of Gina's voice, only to get angry all over again.

What the hell was happening to him?

When it came to that damned woman, he seemed to be cursed.

Nine

Garrett mopped the sweat from his brow and swatted at a bothersome mosquito that wouldn't leave him alone. Walking through the orchard, he paused and looked back at the main house where patches of light glowed from the windows as dusk settled over these vast acres he'd worked so hard to keep in the family name. "I think I might have made a mistake," he admitted to no one in particular, though he realized he was thinking of Laura again. God, he missed her and at times like this, when he needed help wrestling with a decision, the ache within him was raw; as if she'd left this earth just yesterday rather than years earlier.

The old dog that was padding after him whined and Garrett reached down to scratch the shepherd's ears.

"Yes," he said, imagining his wife's encouraging smile. "Don't get me wrong, I think it was a good idea to find all our grandsons, but I didn't expect some of the complications. Jordan Baxter's making noise that he was cheated out of this place and I have a feeling he's not going to rest easy about it. There'll be trouble, sure as shootin'." Garrett snorted and the muscles in the back of his neck tightened. "I don't really know why he's so angry, but it seems as if Jordan thinks he was owed the place, that his uncle promised it to him on his sixteenth birthday."

Garrett straightened and looked at the first stars beginning to wink overhead. "If that's true—which I doubt—it was a long time ago and Cameron Baxter must've changed his mind or he wouldn't have sold it to our family. Hell, it's a mess…" He reached into his shirt pocket for a nonexistent pack of cigarettes, an old habit as he'd quit smoking years before.

"That's not the worst of it," he admitted as he started along a trail leading back to the house. "It's Trent. He's got something going with Gina. I see the way they look at each other, even caught them getting cozy up on the ridge the other day and then just yesterday I surprised them. They were alone in the barn and well, you know…" A wistful smile tugged at the corners of his mouth. "They remind me of us, Laura. The way I couldn't keep my hands off you." He sighed, remembering how hot and randy he'd been at Trent's age.

He passed by an open window of the ranch house and country music, punctuated by static, reached his ears.

"Trouble is," he went on, "Trent's never been one to settle down. Too much of his daddy's blood in his veins, I reckon, so I'm afraid someone's going to get hurt… and it won't be our grandson."

His eyebrows slammed together at the thought. As he was nearly at the house, he quit speaking out loud. He'd have trouble explaining that he was talking to his dead wife, so he clamped his mouth shut, but he was still concerned. Trent and Gina were involved—no question about it—and though the relationship in and of itself wasn't a problem, Garrett was just sick at the thought that Trent might break Gina's heart. That spunky redhead deserved a whole lot better.

On top of all that, Trent and his brother Blake didn't seem to get along. They looked identical, but were, in fact, as different as night to day.

Yes, he thought as he walked up the steps to the back porch and the scent of early blooming roses from the overgrown garden reached his nostrils, things were only going to get worse. At the back door he inched off one boot with the toe of another.

In the next few days the rest of Larry's boys would arrive.

Contrary to what he'd hoped, the homecoming might not be filled with brotherly love. In fact, considering the escalating tension in the house between Trent, Gina and Blake, and the gossip in town running rampant about Larry's illegitimate offspring, to say nothing of Jordan Baxter's determination to make trouble, it was probably a damned good bet that all hell was about to break loose.

The door to her room was ajar and the sounds at night were becoming familiar. The old clock in the foyer ticked off the seconds, a television, the sound low, rumbled down the hallway, and Trent's voice, muted as he was on the phone in the den, was barely audible. He'd insisted on installation of extra telephone lines. Between the running of the ranch, Trent's business and hers, a single line hadn't cut it. Now, because Garrett had agreed and three extra lines had been installed just this past week, faxes could get through while he was on-line and talking on the telephone all at the same time. Garrett hadn't objected as he hoped several of his newfound grandsons would stay on at the ranch for the summer. Most of them would have to conduct their business from the ranch.

All in all, it was a nightmare, Gina thought as she sat on her bed and rubbed the kinks from her neck. She'd spent the past several days trying—and failing—to avoid Trent. They'd shared meals together, bumped into each other in the house, and while she'd helped Suzanne in the kitchen, he and Blake had pitched in whenever Rand had needed an extra hand or two. He'd spent a lot of time in the den and so she'd taken to working from her room.

She'd passed him in the hallways, tried to smile and act nonchalant, but there was always more between them than a cursory nod or "Hello," "How's it goin'?" or even "Did you sleep okay?"

Just yesterday she'd found him alone in the barn when she'd been searching for Garrett.

"Garrett?" she'd called, stepping into the darkened interior that smelled of dry hay and cattle.

"Don't think he's here." Trent's voice had startled her and he'd stepped out of the shadows. His boot heels, ringing on hundred-year-old floorboards as he approached, echoed through the chambers of Gina's fluttering heart. "I'm looking for him myself."

"Oh." She hadn't been able to conjure up a ghost of a smile as a barn owl, disturbed, had hooted from the rafters and dust motes had swirled and danced, appearing golden in the shaft of daylight piercing a solitary round window. She'd looked into his face and her breath had suddenly lost itself between her lungs and her throat. Bladed cheekbones, square jaw, and thick eyebrows guarding eyes so blue that even in the half light she swallowed hard.

"Not in the stables, either. I checked."

"Then…then maybe he went into town."

"His truck's here." He'd been so close she could smell the hint of his aftershave, all male and musk as it mingled with the other odors of the barn.

"Then I'll check the bunkhouse."

"Wait." He'd reached for her hand and as his fingers had caught her wrist a shock had run up her nerves. Sweat had beaded between her shoulder blades. "I think I've been a little rough on you."

"Rough?"

He'd frowned and she'd wanted to kiss those blade-thin lips. Frustration and bewilderment, emotions she didn't normally attribute to him, had been drawn into the lines of his face. "I don't think so."

"The truth is, you bother me, Gina. I don't know what to do with you."

She'd laughed nervously. "Nothing. There's nothing to do."

"No?" He hadn't been convinced, his thick eyebrows cinching together as the owl hooted again, flapped its wings and hid deeper in the rafters.

Oh, if he would just quit touching her. But his fingers had been warm on the inside of her wrist and the air between them had seemed to grow thicker still, heavy with unspoken emotions. She'd immediately thought of their lovemaking, of the fact that she might be pregnant and wanted to confide in him. But she hadn't—she couldn't. Not until she was certain. Maybe not even then. As if he'd read the doubts in her mind, he'd tugged gently on her arm, pulled her closer. His head bent and his lips had hovered over hers in delicious enticement. "I—"

With a creak of hinges the sliding door was suddenly rolled back. As sunlight streamed through the opening, Gina had pulled her hand away from Trent's. She'd turned quickly to find Garrett, Blake and Rand just outside. "That's right, I think we should check with the vet, make sure we have all the serums for inoculations," Garrett had been saying as the bright light flooded the barn's interior. Gina had tried to appear calm and Trent had actually stepped forward.

"Gina and I have been lookin' for you," he'd said without preamble, as if he wasn't the least bit disconcerted that once again they'd been discovered in a nearly compromising position. "I took a call from Wayne, he wants you to get in touch with him, and Gina—" He'd turned to her and with a cocky half smile, said, "She needed something, as well." Raising a dark eyebrow, encouraging her to take over, he'd cocked his head toward the three men as they'd walked inside.

Her mind had gone blank. For the life of her she hadn't been able to remember why she'd been searching for the elder Kincaid.

"Somethin' up?" Garrett had asked. Rand had walked past them and into the barn, Blake had smothered a knowing smile, and Gina, fighting the urge to slap Trent for tossing the ball in her direction, had forced her head to nod and hoped to high heaven that her face was still in the shadows, that her blush was hidden.

"It not that important if you're busy. I just wanted to ask you some questions about Larry—where he was about a year and a half ago. I mean, I know he spent some time with you and Wayne going over this place, so he was here in Whitehorn, but I wondered about side trips he might have taken." They'd been over this territory before, but she'd wanted to double-check her notes, and Garrett was the best source of information she had.

"Just give me a minute and I'll meet you up at the

house," he'd said. The owl had flapped his wings, shedding feathers that had drifted to the floor as Gina, embarrassed all over again, though she'd told herself she was being overly sensitive, had walked stiffly back to the house.

Garrett hadn't been able to shed any more light on Larry's whereabouts during the time when the seventh son had been conceived, nor had he brought up either time he'd caught Gina and Trent embracing. But he wasn't happy about the situation; Gina's feminine intuition was working overtime these days and she sensed Garrett's disapproval.

"Great," she muttered as she pulled one leg under her and leaned against the wall. Well, she didn't have much more time here. The other sons were due to start rolling into the ranch in the morning and if she could just locate that last one, or prove that he didn't exist, she could hightail it. Garrett wanted her to meet all of the men she'd located; she wasn't sure that was such a fabulous idea. Look what had happened when she'd made the mistake of accepting a drink from Trent. One thing had led to another and now…

Oh, she couldn't, wouldn't, dwell on the consequences of that first fateful meeting. Not while she had so much to do. Using her pencil, she scratched her head where the rubber band of her ponytail pulled tight. She spread the files she'd made of each of Larry's offspring beside her on the wrinkled covers. On the desk, her laptop glowed ghostly blue.

Where was that baby?

She'd spent days trying to track him down, to no avail. She had, again, come up dry.

"So much for your sharp investigative mind," she muttered to herself, wondering if there really was a seventh illegitimate son. She flipped open the journal. Could it be a hoax? Did some woman try to pawn off her baby as Larry's to scare him, or to shake him down? Was it all a twisted, cruel joke? Larry Kincaid had certainly used and cheated on any woman he'd contacted, maybe someone had just turned the tables on him.

She tapped her eraser against her teeth and ignored the sound of Trent's laughter rolling up the stairs. She wondered who he was talking to, then reminded herself she didn't care.

"Think," she admonished, and flipped through her notes about the other brothers, scanning the files, searching desperately for some thread that might tie them together, some reason Larry chose the women he did, a commonality aside from the fact that they were all Larry Kincaid's sons. Maybe she would then come up with the most likely candidate for Larry's last fling. She sensed that the woman lived around here in Whitehorn. Larry had been here about the time the child had been conceived.

If he'd been conceived, she reminded herself as she propped a shoulder against the wall.

Each of her reports, typed neatly, dated, cross-referenced and tucked into manila files, gave a short bio on Garrett's grandsons. She had also included a picture of each of the grown men and kept color copies for herself.

She opened a file. The firstborn, Adam Benson, was thirty-seven years old and an overachiever who had earned an MBA and a reputation for having a chip on his shoulder the size of Montana. There were reasons for his anger—deep-seated and dark. Gina studied the picture she'd culled from his college yearbook. Arrogantly handsome with jet-black hair, steely gray eyes and strong, chiseled features vaguely reminiscent of his grandfather's, Adam was a striking man. He'd worked hard and was determined to leave his mark on this world. Always pushing, never satisfied, he'd become a corporate raider and, even at the age of twenty-three as he stared into the camera, he looked the part.

Gina set his page aside and picked up the next, that of thirty-five-year-old Cade Redstone. Gina smiled. Cade was about as opposite from his older brother as he could be, a real, doggie-chasing, bronc-riding, spur-jangling cowboy whose mother, Mariah Raintree, was a Native American who had once worked as a maid for the Kincaids. The snapshot showed Cade at a rodeo in Texas, astride an ornery Brahman bull. His dark eyes gleamed with anticipation. His bronzed skin gleamed with sweat. Gina suspected Cade would feel right at home on the ranch and would probably give his uptight, older half brother a well-deserved ribbing. While Gina expected Adam to turn on a polished leather heel and leave the Whitehorn ranch immediately upon landing, she suspected Cade would dig his cowboy boots into the gravel, grass and dirt of the spread with gusto and fire.

She set his file aside and picked up the third, that of Brandon Harper, the result of Larry's affair with a Las Vegas showgirl. Brandon's stepfather had been a monster and the boy had lashed out, been placed in foster care, adopted, but had been a juvenile delinquent on a path straight to jail. Luckily he'd been athletic and, under the guidance of a coach or two, had avoided jail. He, like Trent, had made his millions on his own.

The photo she'd found of Brandon had been taken just last year at a social event in Lake Tahoe. Dressed in a black tuxedo with a teal vest, he was standing in the foyer of a high-rise hotel, an illuminated fountain spraying upward as a backdrop, a gorgeous model clinging like a piece of expensive jewelry to one arm. Brandon's smile was as cold as his ice-blue eyes. A Rolex watch peeked from beneath his sleeve and his black hair had been perfectly cut. His features were sharp, bold and guarded. While the woman he was with fairly beamed, Brandon looked as if he had ice water running through his veins.

Gina tossed his folder aside and shook her head. This was getting her nowhere in a hurry. The common link between these half brothers was their good looks, very different yet hinting of a Native American ancestry hidden deep in their gene pool. Their mothers were all beautiful, but from different walks of life. Adam's biological mother had been a cheerleader who had died while giving him birth. Cade's, a pretty housekeeper.

Brandon's, a flashy dance hall girl. Young and beautiful and obviously not immune to Larry Kincaid's charms, whatever they had been.

The next file was a double. The Remmington twins. Blake and Trent. Gina's foolish, foolish heart twisted a bit. Living this near to Trent was a mistake. Each night she tossed and turned, thinking of him lying next door. She remembered their lovemaking in the DeMarco Hotel in Dallas and the other times he'd kissed her, his lips seeming to brand her own.

"Don't even go there," she warned herself, but her mind was already wandering from the job at hand to the feel of his skin against hers, the warmth of his hands, the magic of his breath against her flesh.

She swallowed hard and opened the file. Two pictures of nearly identical men stared back at her. Blake was dressed in a white lab coat with a stethoscope slung around his neck. A bright-eyed boy of about three was seated on Blake's bent knee. The floppy-haired imp sported a cast that ran down a chubby leg and he grinned widely as he clutched a one-eyed teddy bear to his chest.

Blake obviously enjoyed his career and the children he cared for. She wondered why, during his marriage, he'd never become a father.

Her stomach clenched at the thought. How ironic that she might be carrying Trent's child. She glanced at her watch, checked the date and sighed. This wasn't how she'd planned to become a mother and yet the thought that a baby—Trent's baby—might be growing inside her was exhilarating. She hadn't thought much about settling down but she'd always wanted children.

And yet she was terrified. The fact that she hadn't yet made the time to buy a pregnancy test convinced her that she was in major denial.

She looked down at the file folder to Trent's picture. It was a far cry from his brother's. Oh, their features were nearly identical, but that was where the likeness ended. Everything about them from their personalities to their attitude toward life appeared to be in diametric opposition to each other.

The snapshot said it all. Trent stood in front of a gusher, a brazen slash of a smile cutting through two days' worth of dark beard. His eyes were blue and triumphant, his hair longer than the current trend and blowing in the breeze. No hard hat for the owner of the company. Pride was etched into the set of his jaw, naked challenge flared in his eyes as he stood, arms folded over his chest, the tails of his denim shirt flapping in the wind. Rugged. Wild. A force to be reckoned with, Trent Remmington was at home in designer suits or faded jeans, a man, she was afraid, she could so easily learn to love.

She gasped. *Love?* She thought she could *love* him? Now where did that ludicrous thought well from? She barely knew the man, for crying out loud, and just because…just because she thought she might be carrying his… Her stomach clenched and she suddenly had trouble breathing. She'd always been a reasonable woman and not one to think that sexual attraction necessarily meant love. But if she was pregnant—

Rap! Rap! Rap!

She glanced up and found Blake leaning against the doorjamb. "Want to take a break?" he asked.

"A break?"

"I've got to drive into town and could use a little company. Besides, you know the town and can point me in the direction of the nearest grocery store. I promised Suzanne I'd pick up some of the supplies she forgot earlier."

"What about Trent?" Gina asked, dumbfounded.

"He's busy." Blake's smile was positively infectious. "Besides, you're prettier."

"I—I don't know," she started, then decided why not? She was getting nowhere fast as it was. "Sure. Just give me a minute."

"I'll meet you in the foyer." He disappeared and she told herself that any personal involvement with any of the Kincaid sons was a mistake, but then, she'd already made the worst of all. She yanked the rubber band from her hair, swiped at the wavy red locks with a brush, slapped some lipstick over her lips and grabbed her purse. Slinging the strap over her shoulder, she breezed down the stairs, nearly running into Trent in the process.

It was funny, she thought, that no matter how much the twins looked alike, she knew instantly which one she was facing and it wasn't just a matter of clothes—nope, it was attitude.

"Going somewhere?" he asked, stopping on the stairs.

"Into town."

His lips compressed. "With Blake." It wasn't a question.

"He wanted me to point out the some of the sights."

"That should take all of two minutes."

"You could come along," she invited with a lift of her shoulder.

His eyes narrowed a fraction. "I'll take a rain check. Have fun."

Was he being sarcastic? Probably. Trent continued up the stairs and Gina sped down the remainder of the flight.

"That's the Branding Iron, a local nightspot," Gina said as Blake steered his plush car through the streets of downtown Whitehorn. Melodic notes of soft jazz whispered through the speakers and the leather interior smelled new.

Blake hitched his chin toward the bar as they passed. "Ever been inside?"

"Just once, to interview the bartender and waitresses. Your father—"

"If you're talking about Larry, let's call him by his name, okay. 'Father' just doesn't seem to fit."

She snorted. "I heard the same thing from Trent."

"So it really is true—great minds do think alike," he joked as he drove past Whitehorn Memorial Hospital and the statue of Lewis and Clark positioned near the front of the building. Tall cottonwoods surrounded the structure and street lamps illuminated the grounds. "I'd always thought that was a fallacy."

"Take a right here." She pointed to the next corner.

"Voilà," he said as the grocery store appeared. Two pickups, a dented station wagon with duct tape holding a taillight together and a Mercedes convertible were parked in the asphalt lot. As Blake cut the engine, a tall, silver-haired man in a sharply pressed suit strode out of the store. Anger and something else—desperation?—pinched the corners of his mouth and he swept the Acura a dark look. In one arm he toted a single paper bag of groceries, but his shoulders were bent with the load of his bad attitude.

"Jordan Baxter," Gina said as Jordan pressed his keyless lock and the lights of his convertible turned on. Opening the door, he slid behind the wheel.

"Who's he?"

"A man you want to avoid. The bad blood between the Baxters and the Kincaids goes back for generations."

Blake laughed. "A family feud. Like the Montagues and Capulets?"

"Not quite so highbrow," she said, smiling at his Shakespearean reference. "More like the Hatfields and the McCoys, I'm afraid."

"Are you? That surprises me. You look like the kind of woman who's not afraid of anything."

"There is no such animal," she said as Jordan threw his Mercedes into reverse. The convertible's sleek finish appeared nearly liquid in the incandescent glow of the street lamps. With a well-tuned roar, the Mercedes took off.

She reached for the door handle, but Blake didn't move. He was fiddling with his key chain with one hand, the fingers of the other hand still poised on the wheel. "Before we go inside," he said, "I'd like to ask you something."

Her muscles stiffened. His teasing attitude had disappeared along with his boyish smile. "Shoot."

"Okay." Turning his head to stare at her directly, he asked, "Are you in love with my brother?"

Ten

Blake's question followed Gina around like a lost puppy. *Are you in love with my brother?* Who knew? She'd managed to laugh at his suggestion and hurry out of the car into the store, but the thought that she might be in love with Trent kept nipping at her heels, trailing after her, interrupting last night's sleep and waking her in the predawn hours. She'd given up on sleep and decided to face the day. But even now as she stepped out of the shower into the steamy bathroom, her mind spun at the thought that she just might be falling in love.

"Get a grip," she told herself, for today was the day that the sons of Larry Kincaid were due to arrive. All her efforts at locating them would culminate this very morning. She flung a thick peach-colored towel around her body, tucked it over her breasts and used a wash cloth to wipe the steam that had collected on the mirror.

Soon enough she could leave Whitehorn, Montana.

And what then?

Click.

The latch on the door sprang and the door itself opened with a loud creak. Holding the towel to her chest, she whirled around. Trent, fully dressed in jeans and a cream-colored shirt with the sleeves rolled up, slipped in. Her towel nearly fell to the cracked linoleum.

"What do you think you're doing?" she demanded in a harsh whisper, her heart hammering wildly.

"I wish I knew."

"What do you mean?"

In answer, he kicked the door shut, latched the lock, then grabbed her. Steam rose in the tiny room lit only by a single bulb in a tulip-shaped fixture over the mirror.

"Are you crazy?" What had gotten into him?

"Probably."

"Now wait a minute—"

"No." His eyes held hers for half a heartbeat and she was lost. She gulped. His lips crashed down on hers and though she wanted to protest, she couldn't call up a solitary word of refusal. No, damn it, she practically melted. Just like the silly kind of woman she detested. As if of their own accord, her arms slipped around his neck and she willingly opened her mouth to him. She closed her eyes, feeling soft droplets of water drip from the ringlets of her wet hair onto her bare shoulders.

She was crazy. Downright certifiable. And yet she kissed him as eagerly as he did her. She told herself that she was only fanning the fires of a passion that should never have been lit in the first place, but she didn't care. What harm there was had already been done.

Her towel slipped a bit, edging lower, but she was so caught up in the emotion of the moment, she didn't feel it surrender to the insistent pull of gravity, nor would she have cared. Trent was kissing her, devouring her, and deep inside she heated, her flesh tingling, her breath shallow and raspy as she pretended they were all alone in the universe and that loving Trent Remmington was forever her destiny.

Her eyes fluttered a second then closed in ecstasy as he lowered his mouth, kissing the crook of her neck and tugging the towel down until her breasts were exposed. She moaned and leaned against the sink as he bared one round nipple and a cool current of air from the open window moved across her skin. Her nipples puckered in anticipation.

He, running a thumb over one breast, teased and played with the rosy little bud of the other with his tongue, teeth and lips until desire pumped liquid fire through Gina's veins. Hot. Raw. Hungry. She lolled her head back, her hands at her sides, her fingers gripping the porcelain sink as her knuckles grew white. She wanted him—more than any reasonable woman would hunger for a man. The ache deep inside her pulsed in white-hot beats that pounded through her brain and evoked a whispered moan from her throat.

Somewhere in the back of her mind she knew that she should stop him. On this day of days, when the house would soon be crawling with Kincaids, she needed to be composed and relaxed, cool and collected. But his tongue was liquid magic, stroking, touching, caressing. The serrated edges of his teeth toyed with her skin and she arched closer to him, wanting more.

"That's it, love," he said, and slowly pulled the towel away from her to let it pool on the bathroom floor. Steamy mist hung in the air as he settled onto his knees, his mouth easing lower, his tongue rimming her navel, his hands moving over her abdomen. Calloused fingers smoothed her skin and she thought of the baby that might be growing within her.

His child.

His breath was hot against the damp nest of curls at the apex of her legs. He kissed her there and she moaned again, her skin on fire. With little urging, she opened to him and he kissed her, softly at first, then with more insistence, his lips and tongue sucking and licking, his breath swirling hot within her.

She bit her lip to keep from screaming, felt him lift her legs over his shoulders as she balanced against the sink. His groan reverberated through her, and the entire universe seemed to center deep in the most feminine part of her. As a morning breeze swept through the cracked-open window, chasing away the last remaining wisps of mist, the pressure mounted. Sweat sheened her body. His fingers dug into her skin. Lifted higher and higher, she was climbing, gasping, panting, until she reached the brink and fell over. Her entire body convulsed, the cold porcelain pressed into her hips, the heat of the man she loved breathing fire deep inside.

"Oooohh." Her throat was dry, her skin fevered. She couldn't think, could barely speak. "Trent…oh, Trent."

"Shh, baby, it's okay." His words pulsed through her.

"No…I… Ooooh!" She bucked again and the universe collided. Her hands grabbed his head and held him close. She squeezed her eyes shut and clamped her mouth against the primal scream that threatened to roar from her.

And then it was over. Her body went limp as he slowly let her legs fall back to the floor. She was dizzy, still spinning.

Straightening, climbing to his feet, Trent dragged her close and wrapped his strong arms around her to cradle her while she drooped against him and pressed her face into his denim-draped shoulder. Spasm after spasm rocketed through her and for a brief second the bathroom seemed to tilt. Standing in bare feet, she clung to him, dripping in sweat, still aching from his lovemaking.

"What— Why…why did you come in here?" she said when some of her equilibrium slowly returned.

"I thought I just showed you."

"Yes, but…I mean…" She rocked away from him and scraped her hair from her eyes with one hand. "Why now?"

"Because you've been avoiding me."

"You noticed."

"Hard not to."

Oh, God, she was stark naked! Reason swept back with a vengeance and she groaned. "I need to get dressed."

"Fine." He flipped down the lid of the toilet and took a seat.

"What? You can't stay here. It's indecent. Someone might see…" He arched an insolent dark eyebrow and she sighed, realizing the point was moot. "Fine. Whatever." She stepped into her panties and hooked her bra behind her back while trying not to notice that he was studying her for all he was worth. "Kind of a reverse strip show, isn't it?"

His Cheshire-cat grin was insufferable. He stacked his hands behind his head insolently. "Maybe later I can rewind the tape and watch it the right way."

"In your dreams."

"Precisely." Her head snapped up to see if he was teasing but his expression was as sober as if he'd been confessing to a priest. His laser-blue gaze burned into hers.

Instantly the heat in her cheeks ignited. She swallowed hard and looked away. What was going on here? Besides acting out some kind of sexual fantasy. Was there more? Or was it her all-too-active imagination? Snatching her shorts and blouse from a hook near the door, she quickly dressed and then, praying that the hallway was empty, unlocked the door and poked her head out.

All clear. She scooped up her nightgown.

"Not so fast." Trent's voice arrested her.

"What?" She glanced over her shoulder.

"What did you and Blake talk about last night?" Now she was imagining just a trace of jealousy in his gaze. Was it possible?

"Everything and nothing. Your name came up."

"I hope in the 'everything' category."

Blake's question ricocheted through her brain again. *Are you in love with my brother?* Her throat was suddenly as dry as the Mojave Desert. She had to get away. "What do you think?" she quipped back at him, her hand on the doorknob again.

"What I think, Gina, is that you're running scared." His words stopped her cold.

"From?"

But she knew the answer before she opened the door and walked briskly along the hallway.

"Me, darlin'. You just don't know what to do with me," he said loudly enough that the words chased her all the way downstairs.

Amen, she thought. *If I live to be older than Methuselah, I'll never have the first idea of how to handle you.*

Seated around the cold hearth in the living room of the main house, Trent surveyed the newcomer with a jaundiced eye. He was the first of the next batch of Larry's bastards to show up. Dressed in clean, dark jeans, a plaid shirt and a pair of snakeskin cowboy boots, he'd introduced himself as Mitch Fielding. From the small talk that had erupted, Trent learned that Mitch was the youngest of Larry's bastards.

Mitch was a construction worker who lived nearby. A widower with twin six-year-old girls, Mitch was about six feet tall, with sandy hair, tanned skin and intense hazel eyes. He seemed eager to meet Garrett and the rest of the brood and his aw-shucks, rural persona gritted on Trent's nerves. The guy even blushed when he'd met Gina, and Trent had been certain Mitch would wear the toe of his boot out with the shy, country-boy routine. It was enough to make Trent sick, but then, he'd been acting way out of character ever since he'd met Gina.

Any man who looked at her was a potential rival.

Now, as Mitch, seated on the worn couch, gushed on about his daughters and Gina sat with Garrett and Blake listening in rapt interest, Trent wanted to plant himself next to her, throw an arm around her shoulders just to make sure that any and all males who looked in her direction knew she was off the market.

Or was she?

Never in his life had he been confused about a woman, but this one, Gina, made him think twice. He hadn't been this possessive of any woman, not even Beverly when she'd told him she was carrying his child.

His jaw grew hard and he touched the ancient rifle mounted over the mantel, running an experienced finger down the dark barrel of the weapon. For a moment he thought of this morning when he'd heard Gina rise and dash into the bathroom. He hadn't been able to keep himself from following her. He'd planned to just talk to her but she'd been so damned sexy in the steamy room, her wet red hair framing a fresh face devoid of makeup. Her green eyes had rounded, her towel had slipped and suddenly he'd forgotten about saying anything. Even now, remembering her thrown back against the counter, her breasts so white and tipped with perfect peach nipples, he started to grow hard. Closing his mind to the erotic memory, he tried to concentrate on the conversation at hand.

"...so I was glad to get the call," Mitch was saying, his fingers laced, his hands hanging between his knees. "My little girls need to know their roots. Their great-grandpa. Their uncles."

Trent's stomach turned sour.

"I agree," Garrett said, casting a knowing look in Trent's direction. "We're family."

Blake laughed. "Kind of an odd mix, but, yeah, we are a family."

Trent wasn't buying it. Not for a minute.

He suspected Larry's legitimate kids, Collin, the man who was about Mitch Fielding's age, and his daughter, Melanie, might not swallow the "one big happy family" fantasy, either.

He hazarded a glance at Gina, caught her gaze for just a second and realized that the reason he was sticking around the ranch wasn't because of Garrett and his half brothers. Other than idle curiosity about them, Trent really didn't give a damn. No, his attraction to the ranch was solely Gina Henderson.

* * *

"…and so once I found out that you all existed, I knew I had to do something," Garrett was saying, standing at the head of the huge dining room table where the newfound illegitimate sons of Larry Kincaid and a few other Kincaid relatives had gathered. All the men had shown up earlier this morning and the tension in the ranch house had been nearly palpable. Strangers who were half brothers, men who had grown up not knowing about their biological father, this ranch, or each other, were understandably wary. Uncomfortable.

Trent was by far the worst.

Half-drunk cups of coffee were scattered over the oak top and a few of the brothers had brought notepads. Trent hadn't. Sitting low in his chair, his arms folded across his chest, he watched the proceedings silently, appearing as if he'd rather be anywhere else on the planet.

Gina had claimed a chair next to Garrett's. The box of paraphernalia and her notes lying open, some tossed around the table as the men perused her work and the mementoes Larry had kept of his children. Adam's report cards; a citation from the juvenile system on Trent; a rodeo ribbon of Cade's; a yearbook with pictures of Brandon scoring half-a-dozen touchdowns; a copy of Blake's application to medical school; a photograph of Mitch and his daughters and, of course, the date book/journal indicating that there was one son missing from the table, a baby boy as yet unlocated—maybe never to be located.

Each man had fumbled through his file and the small pieces of his life that Larry had squirreled away. A range of emotions was on display from wistful smiles to barely controlled rage. Other stares were bored or vacant, as if a silent agony was being reined in.

Gina's throat was tight when she witnessed the pain of rejection some of these men, who all had once been impressionable boys, experienced.

Larry Kincaid should have been castrated, then drawn and quartered for leaving his sons to grow up on their own. But they were here now. And they had questions.

As Garrett spoke, Gina's stomach was in knots. She felt like the proverbial fish out of water. On top of it, she was the reason all these men had been found and found quickly, though, it seemed, there wasn't a whole lot of animosity directed her way.

Except from Trent. He hadn't quite forgiven her for the lies she'd told him in Dallas. Not that she could really blame him, she supposed, but looking at him now, she felt her heart thump deep in her chest. He sat low on his back, regarding everyone with guarded eyes, as if he trusted no one. Which he probably didn't. For a second she thought of this morning, how intimate they'd been, then she looked quickly away and tried to concentrate.

"...so I got together with Wayne here." Garrett motioned to his cousin, seated to his left. Wayne, a lean, wiry man with tanned, lined skin and the same startling blue eyes as Garrett's, half stood and nodded a full head of silvering blond hair. "And along with a few other

people who were involved with this ranch, I decided that
I'd buy it back and divide it between all of you. Until
now Wayne's managed this place, but he lives in town.
Rand Harding's our foreman and he and his wife
Suzanne are occupying the foreman's quarters. They'll
stay on, along with some of the hands who've been
working here for years."

He paused to eye each of his grandsons, then continued. "Now, before you all start talking about not being
interested in the spread, or not needing it or not even
wanting to be bothered ranching, just hold on. I'm
thinking the place will be kind of a touchstone, a place
you can all own and where you can all connect. Those
who want to run it, well, okay, those who want to be
silent partners, that's okay, too." Again he hesitated,
tapped his fingers nervously on the ancient oak table.
"Well, hell, there's no way to say this other than straight
out." He looked at each man in turn. "My son Larry
didn't do right by any of you and I want to make it up
to you and make you feel wanted—all part of the
Kincaid family."

Gina watched the men's faces. They were all serious
now, staring at the man they hadn't known was their
grandfather. Blake and Trent, seated next to each other,
acted as if there was a wall between them.

Adam Benson, the oldest, sat next to Wayne Kincaid.
Gina wasn't sure she liked the brooding man who hadn't
bothered hiding his arrogance. She could well believe
that he was a corporate raider by trade. He was wearing

a starched white shirt, power tie and sleek navy-blue business suit. Hawklike, he silently observed the scene around him, and Gina could almost see the wheels turning in his mind.

On the opposite side of the table, Mitch Fielding tapped work-roughened fingers on the arm of his chair. His expression was serene, as if all the melodrama of his biological father didn't bother him a bit. With sandy-brown hair, streaked by hours working under the sun, and hazel eyes that were warm and filled with energy, Mitch seem to accept what Garrett and Wayne proposed without much concern. His plaid shirt was clean but worn, his jeans, too, had seen better days, yet he was as unconcerned about his appearance as he seemed about all the fuss about the land.

"You want us all as equal partners?" Adam asked.

"Yes," Garrett said as Wayne nodded.

Adam leaned forward. "Once you called, I did a little research on the place. It's held in trust, right? For a Jennifer McCallum—"

"She's a Kincaid, as well," Garrett interjected. "A cousin, like Wayne here."

"I'm one of the trustees," Wayne said, "but we all voted and have agreed to sell the ranch to Garrett. It's unanimous."

"And there are no liens?" Adam asked, his face a study in concentration.

"No." Garrett shook his head.

Wayne agreed. "We'd already decided to sell the

place when Garrett came up with the idea to buy it and give it all to you."

"And you're doing this with no strings attached." Adam's dubious gaze was centered on his grandfather.

"All I ask is that you stay as long as you want, get to know each other, become a part of the family."

"Sounds good to me," Mitch said.

Adam's mouth became a thin line of distrust. "I don't believe in getting something for nothing."

Trent's jaw twitched a bit, as if he'd had the very same thought. He caught Gina's eye, held it for a minute, then leaned back in his chair even further and glanced away.

"I think it's a hell of an idea." Cade Redstone slapped his hand on the table. Gina guessed it took a lot to intimidate this rough-and-tumble cowboy. Ranch-tough, Cade was a strong-willed, no-nonsense man who had traveled all the way from his stepfather's spread in Texas. Cade met Adam's hard glare and didn't back down for a second. "A hell of an idea," he repeated.

"I didn't say it was a bad idea, I just had a few questions."

"As well you should," Garrett cut in, spreading his hands as if he were indeed pouring oil on troubled waters. "As well you should."

"Didn't you sell off twenty acres awhile back to the Laughing Horse reservation?" Adam zeroed in on Wayne.

"That's right. They needed it for a hotel and spa."

"And a casino."

"Maybe," Wayne agreed.

"But it won't have any bearing on the rest of the land?" Adam wasn't convinced.

"That's right," Garrett answered. He leaned forward and impaled his firstborn grandson with his own hard glare.

"Even if it did, we could work things out through the county," Brandon Harper, the second of Larry's sons, thought out loud. He stuck two fingers under his collar and loosened his tie. An investment banker who'd made his fortune on his own, he was used to dealing with property disputes and seemed to relish any kind of battle, be it legal or otherwise. Blue eyes, so much like his grandfather's, held Adam's. He didn't flinch. "It's not a problem," he said with authority.

Adam wasn't about to back down. Underlying currents of tension snapped in the air. Every man in the room had his own personal ax to grind and grind it he would.

"I think Brandon's right." Garrett took charge again. Though the least volatile of any man at the table, he was a force to be reckoned with. "Besides, I didn't call you together to hassle over the legalities of what I'm doing. I just wanted to start us out together, on the same page. Now, Gina here is convinced that there's another boy out there somewhere, a young one, still a baby."

"A boy Larry fathered?" Brandon asked, tossing back a hank of black hair that fell over his eyes.

"Yes." Garrett sighed and tapped his knuckles on the table. "Unless that notation in his journal's a fake. You all saw it there, in the box." He moved his gaze from one grandson to the next. "Now, I'd suggest we all have lunch and get to know each other. I believe Rand and Suzanne have things ready on the back porch."

He scraped his chair back and the others did the same. A few men tried to make small talk. Mitch and Cade were the most outgoing. Blake tried to draw Brandon into conversation while Adam kept to himself and Trent shot Gina a look that reminded her of their encounter in the bathroom. Her skin flushed, but she ignored it and muttered as she passed him, "I think it would be a good idea if you tried to connect with your brothers."

"Half brothers." Scowling, he fell into step with Gina and sighed. "The old man's a fool, you know. All this idealistic, maudlin crap. He feels guilty because his son was a first-class jerk, but that doesn't mean any of us will ever get along or want to have anything to do with each other."

The caustic sound of his words scraped her raw. "It wouldn't hurt you to try, Trent," she said, coming to Garrett's defense swiftly. Pivoting to face him, she poked a finger at the middle of his chest. "And while I'm giving advice, why don't you lose the attitude, okay?" Her voice escalated passionately. "You're damned lucky to know your grandfather and no matter what Larry might have been, Garrett Kincaid is one extremely earnest, decent, hardworking and fair man. Things could be worse. A lot worse. Think about it!"

With that, she marched out of the dining room, not

giving one damn who had heard her outburst. Trent Remmington was the most irritating, exciting, passionate man she'd ever met in her life, but she wasn't going to listen to anyone second-guess Garrett's intentions. And if Adam Benson or any of the other half brothers opened his mouth against Garrett, he'd get a piece of her mind, as well.

Still steaming, she walked through the French doors to a back porch where the afternoon temperature was already climbing. Country music was playing softly from a radio propped on the windowsill. A long picnic table had been covered with a plaid cloth anchored by platters and serving dishes steaming in the shade of the porch's overhang. Suzanne and Rand were smiling as they met Larry's sons. A pretty woman Gina recognized as Janie, a waitress from the Hip Hop Café helped the half brothers load their plates while a weak breeze turned the leaves of the cottonwoods standing guard near the fence line.

The tangy scent of barbecued chicken vied with the aromas of baked beans and garlic bread. Gina's stomach rumbled softly, yet she didn't think she could swallow a single bite. A barrel of ice held soft drinks and bottles of beer, while a coffee urn stood ready at one end of the picnic table. Yellow jackets had already begun buzzing near the overflowing platters, and the dog, ever vigilant, lay just at the edge of the porch, head in his paws, brown eyes bright and expectant as he hoped for a tidbit tossed his way or a scrap to fall to the floor.

"Danged bees," Garrett rumbled, swatting at a pesky yellow jacket that hovered near his head.

"They won't each much," Wayne said.

"They'd better not, or I'll shoot 'em." Rand winked at his wife who rolled her eyes.

"Behave, Rand Harding," Suzanne teased. She glanced at Gina. "I swear sometimes I'm afraid to take him out in public." She touched her husband's chin. "You'd better mind your manners, or I won't let you go to Leanne's wedding." As if she realized Gina might not understand, she scooped up a spoonful of beans and as she plopped them onto a plate added, "Leanne is Rand's younger sister and she's getting married soon. It wouldn't do to have him show what a true bumpkin he is."

"Careful, woman," Rand growled softly, leaning closer to her. "I might just have to show you who's boss."

Suzanne tossed back her head and laughed. Her auburn hair fell down her back in soft waves and a few of the men glanced at her in open admiration. "Oh, right. That'll be the day, cowboy."

Rand's smile was one of wicked amusement and without so much as opening his mouth, he silently conveyed to his wife what he planned to do to her if she tried to tell him what to do. Again, Suzanne laughed in pure, loving delight.

Gina's heartstrings tugged at the playful banter.

"You're the foreman, right?" Cade Redstone, balancing a full plate, asked Rand as he placed a slab of garlic bread on his plate.

Rand nodded. "Yep. You thinkin' about stayin' on?"

"Not just thinkin' about it. I plan to stick around at least for the summer and I want to work. I've been around horses and cattle all my life."

"Consider yourself signed up," Rand said, and clapped Cade on the shoulder.

Trent had sauntered onto the deck and snagged a bottle of beer. Twisting off the top, he started a conversation with Adam Benson.

Well, it was a beginning, Gina supposed.

Gina accepted a plate from Janie, but realized as she smelled the tangy chicken that she wouldn't be able to eat a bite. Her stomach instantly roiled at the sight of the food. She tried to blame it on the tense conversation in the dining room, on the excitement of meeting the men she'd spent days searching for, on being keyed up whenever she was around Trent, but deep inside she suspected her lack of appetite and nausea were from another source.

Enough of this, she thought, angry with herself when she realized that she'd been afraid to find out the truth. It was time to face the future. As soon as possible, come hell or high water, she was going to go into town and stop by the local pharmacy. Once there she'd buy a pregnancy test kit, bring it back to the ranch, and use it. Then she'd know for sure whether or not she was carrying Trent Remmington's baby.

Eleven

"So, you've got it bad for the investigator lady." Blake's comment wasn't a question. He stood, leaning a shoulder on the doorjamb, sipping from a long-necked bottle of beer as the newfound half brothers talked between themselves. They'd eaten, had dessert and were now milling around in smaller groups. Wayne and Garrett were about to take some of the heirs on a tour; Adam Benson had disappeared into the house. Gina had ducked out. Brandon Harper had flung a few questions about family history toward the twins, but was now striking up a conversation with Suzanne Harding, so Blake had cornered Trent.

"What makes you think I've got it bad for anyone?"

"It's written all over your face. You couldn't take

your eyes off of her during that meeting and, remember, I know you. We're the only two people here who share the same mother." Blake's eyes, so much like his own, held his. "Come on, no more B.S. What's up?"

There wasn't much reason to lie. "As you know, I met Gina a few weeks ago," Trent admitted.

"Why don't we drive into town and I'll buy you a real beer at the Branding Iron? You can tell me all about it on the way." He shoved his hair out of his eyes. "While you're at it, maybe you can explain what makes this ranch tick."

"I didn't think you were interested in ranching."

"I wasn't, but I've changed." Blake frowned and picked at the label on his bottle. "Divorce does that."

"You and Elaine were never right for each other."

"Amen." They both drained their bottles and left them on a table. As they walked out the front door they spied Garrett pointing out the bunkhouse, stable, machine sheds and various outbuildings to the sons of Larry who were interested in the ranch.

Trent wasn't certain he was in that particular category, but he wasn't alone. Benson seemed to want no part of his Whitehorn legacy.

As he and Blake walked to his twin's car, Trent slapped at a horsefly that hadn't figured out the herd was in the west pasture. The warmth of a bright Montana sun beat against the back of his neck and he couldn't help but smile when he spied a frantic white-faced calf, bawling and running awkwardly toward the herd in search of his mother.

Trent slid into the passenger seat. He'd never been particularly close to Blake, but wondered for the first time in his life if that had been a mistake.

Blake slipped into the driver's seat and shoved a key into the ignition. "Can you believe Larry Kincaid is our father? I mean, we've had some time to think about it, but never really discussed it." The Acura roared to life.

"Nope. But then, I was never close to Harold." Trent focused on a copse of aspens in one of the fields. Horses stood head to rump in the shade, their tails swatting at flies, their ears pricked. Coats from dun to black gleamed in the sunlight and Trent, for the first time in his life, felt a bonding with the land. But that was bull. He'd never felt anything close to roots in his life. Just as he'd never been able to settle down with one woman. But staring out the window to the stubble of freshly mown fields, Gina's image appeared in his mind's eye— her quick smile, wavy red hair and flashing green eyes.

Blake snorted. "Mom ran Harold ragged when she was alive." He threw the car into reverse, backed up, then jammed it into drive. "I just wish she'd told us about Larry before she died."

"Would've been thoughtful," Trent agreed, not wanting to think too long or hard on the fact that Barbara Simms Remmington had given up her fight with cancer—one final battle that she hadn't won. "But then, Mom always did things her way."

Blake slipped a pair of wraparound sunglasses onto

the bridge of his nose. "Do you think Larry ever thought about contacting us?"

Trent lifted a shoulder. "Who knows? Garrett told me there was a letter once, one that she wrote sometime after she found out she was going to die." He cleared his throat. "Supposedly she told Larry about us but warned him to keep his distance because we'd grown up to be fine young men or some such trash and didn't want him messing things up."

Blake's hands tightened on the wheel as he attempted to avoid potholes in the rutted lane. Long, dry grass brushed the undercarriage of the low-slung car. "Guess he took her advice," Trent observed.

"Probably didn't want to be bothered with a couple more kids."

"Fine guy, our father."

"The best." Blake slowed for the highway, saw no traffic and gunned it. The Acura sprang forward, wheeling onto the main road, tires spinning gravel before connecting with asphalt.

"So where is this letter?"

Trent lifted a shoulder. "Who knows? I didn't see it in that Pandora's box that Celia—er, Gina passed around today."

Blake's eyes narrowed as he stared through his dark lenses and punched in the radio. Smooth jazz filtered through the speakers. "You called Gina 'Celia'?"

Trent's jaw hardened. It was just like his brother to pick up on any little error. "Just a mistake."

Raising a dark eyebrow identical to his twin's, Blake said, "Better be careful and keep your women straight. One doesn't like to be called by another's name."

"How would you know?" Trent asked, irritated at his brother all over again. That was the trouble with Blake. Any time Trent had felt the slightest bit of brotherly affection for him, Blake would do something anal and irritating and self-righteous. It was enough to remind Trent that he was better off fending for himself.

"Oh, believe me, I know," Blake said, and Trent had a glimmer that there was more to his brother than met the eye, a darker side filled with his own secrets. Well, well, well. They pulled up behind a tractor chugging down the road while pulling a trailer stacked high with hay bales. Blake eased into the oncoming lane, punched it, and the Acura surged past the farmer to settle back into the right lane and eat up the miles.

"I thought you were always a one-girl guy," Trent said as they neared the town.

"For the most part," Blake hedged, and didn't elaborate as he took a corner a little too fast and the tires whined. "But you weren't." He drove over a final rise and the town of Whitehorn appeared, rising out of the ranch land in a cluster of old and new buildings. "So now we're back to it," Blake said, easing off the accelerator as they passed a Welcome To Whitehorn sign followed closely by a new speed limit. "What's the deal with Gina?"

* * *

Gina eyed the home pregnancy tests on a shelf in the town pharmacy, decided they were all about the same and tucked a box under her arm. Though she hardly knew anyone in the store, she stupidly felt self-conscience, as if she were wearing a bright neon sign that said she thought she might be pregnant.

"Get over it," she mumbled to herself. People took the tests every day.

But not you. Until last month, you were a twenty-seven-year-old virgin.

Ignoring the gibe, she grabbed a tube of toothpaste, a roll of film, the latest edition of the *Whitehorn Journal* and a bottle of shampoo, then walked to the register. The cashier, who was barely eighteen from the looks of her, was snapping gum and blinking as if she was just getting used to contacts. She took an eternity ringing up the items.

The pharmacist, standing on a raised platform behind a half wall displaying over-the-counter medications, vitamins and herbs, was busily filling prescriptions. Throughout the store country music was playing softly over the whir of ceiling fans.

Shifting from one foot to the other, Gina had her wallet out of her purse and wondered if anyone in Whitehorn had ever heard of merchandise scanners. A skinny man in rimless glasses and smelling as if he hadn't bathed in this century got in line behind her, and another girl, one Lily Mae had pointed out to her as Christina Montgomery, clutching more hair-care and beauty products than she could hold without a basket, stood a few feet from the smelly man.

Eventually the girl at the register had totaled up her bill and sang out the amount. Gina fished in her wallet and came up with a couple of bills.

"Have a nice day," the girl at the register intoned automatically as she handed Gina her change.

"You, too." Gina scooped up her bag and, hoping the damned pregnancy test wasn't visible through the white paper, spied Winona Cobbs flipping through the magazine rack. That was the trouble with a small town, a person couldn't help but run into someone she knew. With a quick smile and wave in Winona's direction, Gina beelined past the latest in foot balms, bath oil beads and denture cleansers to the front door.

Outside the sun was bright, the afternoon warm. It had been nearly an hour since the gathering of Kincaid brothers had begun to splinter apart.

When she'd spied Trent with Blake, nursing beers and surveying the countryside, Gina had run upstairs, grabbed her purse and hightailed it outside to her Explorer, only pausing long enough to make a quick excuse to Garrett. Then she'd driven like a madwoman into town. Her pulse had been hammering, a headache pounding behind her eyes. She'd almost felt guilty, like a convict on the run, as she'd pushed the speed limit through the hills on her way into town.

How foolish. Now, balancing her bag, Gina reached into the purse slung over her shoulder and slipped a pair of sunglasses onto her nose. Searching for her keys, she looked into a deep pocket, not paying attention as she rounded a corner and slammed into a man walking in the opposite direction.

"Oh!" She nearly stumbled. The newspaper dropped from beneath her arm and the bag from the pharmacy slipped from her fingers. Large male hands grabbed her shoulders, keeping her upright, and with a sinking sensation she realized she'd just run smack-dab into Trent Remmington.

She dropped her keys and they jangled as they hit the cement.

Oh, God. The pregnancy test! "I—I didn't see you," she stammered as she felt her face turn a dozen shades of red.

Pull yourself together, Gina.

"I figured that," he said dryly, and to her mortification she realized he wasn't alone. Blake was just a step behind. Blake reached down, stuffed the toothpaste and film that had spilled onto the sidewalk into the bag and handed the sorry-looking sack with its contents back to her.

Gina scrambled for the keys glinting in the sunlight.

"Fancy running into you," she quipped, managing what she hoped appeared to be a nonchalant smile though her heart was drumming a million beats a second. What if he saw the pregnancy test, guessed that she thought she might be carrying his baby? "I, um, I thought I already told you we have to quit meeting like this."

Trent released her. "My thoughts exactly," he said dryly,

but no smile toyed at those razor-thin lips. His eyebrows had slammed together and his nostrils flared slightly.

He knew. Oh, God, he knew! "I, um, have to get going. I'll see you back at the ranch."

"I'll look forward to it," Blake said, but he, too, sober as a judge, didn't so much as crack a smile. A horrible, sinking sensation pounded through Gina's already aching head. She was certain that her secret was out. The irony of it was, she didn't know herself if she was pregnant or not.

Garrett had the feeling that something was going to blow. The tension between Gina and Trent was nearly palpable, like the electricity that charges the air just before a thunderstorm breaks.

It was just a matter of time.

He walked to the stables where the smell of horses and dry hay met him. Rand was in the third stall examining a mare who had been favoring a front leg.

"How is she?"

"Ornery," Rand said as he bent the foreleg back and straddled it while keeping one eye on the palomino's head. Though she was tethered, Mandy had been known to take a nip out of man's hide. "As usual." He was poking the inside of the hoof, watching the mare's reaction. As the mare shifted, he growled, "Don't even think about it," then to Garrett, "What's up?"

"Nothing good," Garrett replied as his thoughts turned back to Trent and Gina. It was obvious those two were falling in love, they just didn't know it yet. "I'm going into town later to interview a couple of gals who are interested in doing the cooking out here. One looks pretty good. She's got a son and would like a live-in arrangement. Thought you might pass that information on to Suzanne. Just in case you see her before I do."

"She'll be relieved," Rand admitted. "She's got her hands full with the books, Mack, and Joe."

"How's that son of yours?"

Rand looked up and grinned. Proud as a peacock, he was. "Couldn't be better." The horse shifted and tossed her head. "Oh, no, you don't," Rand said to the mare.

"I'll see you around." Garrett slapped the rail of the stall, then headed outside where the sun was bright. Rubbing the back of his neck, he eyed the parking lot.

The lot was pretty empty. Trent and Blake had driven into town.

So had Gina. Separately.

Probably just a coincidence, and yet the feeling that there was going to be trouble lingered with Garrett as he made his way to his truck. He opened the door and slid into the sun-warmed interior, then poked his key into the ignition. Trent and Gina weren't like oil and water, he decided, ramming the gearshift into reverse, backing up, then nosing the old truck toward the lane. Nope, those two were more like gasoline and a lit match.

A dangerous and extremely volatile combination.

Someone was bound to get burned.

Twelve

The beer didn't settle well in his stomach. Jordan had spent nearly an hour nursing his bottle and his frustration at the bar of the Branding Iron. Besides, he didn't fit in with the blue-collar crowd that was beginning to get off work. Half a dozen mill workers and cowboys had sauntered in, laughing and joking, all wearing dirty jeans and relieved smiles that they'd put in their shifts for the day. Talking to each other and catching the barmaid's attention, they filtered through the front door to take up their usual spots in booths, at the pool table, or here at the bar, already eyeing the television screen mounted high overhead in hopes of viewing the latest sporting event while thirstily tossing back brewskies and nibbling on peanuts before going home to the wife and kids.

Jordan caught a few grim looks cast his way from the men huddled over their drinks. Sour grapes, he thought. These poor working stiffs would never rise above their small-town roots and they were envious of a poor, sickly kid who had. They'd have manure and sawdust on their boots until the day they died. Jordan Baxter had gone from secondhand sneakers to Italian leather loafers.

The door banged open and Christina Montgomery, the mayor's youngest and wildest daughter, flew into the bar. Several of the locals swiveled on their stools to check her out. Petite, curvy, and an outrageous flirt, Christina beelined for the bar. "I'll…I'll have a…" She looked at the bartender and shoved an errant strand of chestnut hair off her face. "A gin and tonic…no…just a…oh, it doesn't matter, a diet soda, I guess!"

"That all?" the bartender asked, and Christina's pouty lips pursed.

"Yeah, yeah, that's all," she said, lifting herself onto a bar stool and, noticing a few male glances cast her way in the reflection of the mirror, she shook out her mane of hair. Dressed in a blue dress with silver earrings dripping from her ears, she accepted her drink, took a sip and scowled.

Jordan saw her glance his way and offer him a cunning smile. He wasn't interested and looked away, but Christina wasn't rebuffed, just turned her attention to a young cowboy seated in a corner booth. His ears actually turned red as he blushed, but Christina didn't stop there. With a walk that drew a man's attention, she took her drink and sauntered slowly to a table near the back of the room. The girl was pure sex and she knew it, flaunted it.

Her father, Mayor Ellis Montgomery, had a major problem on his hands whether he knew it or not. But it wasn't really any of Jordan's business.

He tossed a few bills onto the bar, slid off his stool and realized that he'd been so caught up in his silent anger at the Kincaids, he'd barely touched his drink. Well, he sure as hell wasn't going to down it now. He made his way to the front door.

It opened in his face and two men he'd never seen before stepped inside. In an instant he recognized them as Kincaids. And twins at that. Tall and broad-shouldered, they both had the piercing blue eyes, dark hair, and arrogance that had always run deep in Kincaid blood. Probably a couple of Larry's bastards.

"Excuse me," the one with the less harsh expression said as they passed. He was dressed as if he planned to spend his afternoon at the golf course. *Get real, buddy,* Jordan laughed to himself, *there ain't no country club here in Whitehorn.* The other one, in faded jeans and a shirt with rolled-up sleeves, didn't say a word, just gave Jordan a cursory glance that made his blood boil.

Jordan couldn't help himself. "Don't tell me," he said, "Kincaids."

Mr. Nice Guy nodded and smiled. "Looks that way. Blake Remmington." He extended his hand and added, "My brother, Trent."

Jordan ignored the fingers stretching in his direction. "Just give the old man a word of advice. He can't sell something that isn't his."

The hand fell. "Pardon me?"

"You heard me."

"Who're you?" The arrogant one was narrowing his eyes suspiciously.

"Garrett Kincaid's worst nightmare."

The twins exchanged glances, then smiled as if in on a private secret.

Jordan's blood boiled.

"Are you the local town thug?" the hard-ass named Trent asked. "If you are, you'd better get some new threats."

"Just give him the message."

Trent looked ready to jump down Jordan's throat. *Good. Take your best shot, bastard, I'll have you up on assault charges so fast your head will spin.*

The cooler one, Blake he'd said his name was, placed his hand over his brother's arm, as if to restrain him. "Look, Mr....Baxter, is it? I don't know what your beef is, but peddle it someplace else, okay? We're not interested."

That did it. Jordan's barely reined-in temper snapped. "You will be," Jordan said, and shouldered open the door.

Yep, they were bastards, both of them. Jordan couldn't make his way out of this joke of a watering hole fast enough.

Outside, he breathed deep of the fresh air, then

squinted against the sunlight and tried to shake off the knowledge that he should have held his tongue. Warning the Kincaids was a mistake. It was better to strike first, be a coral snake rather than a rattler. No reason to tip his hand, such as it was, but running into Larry's bastard twins, he'd been blindsided and wanted to lash out. He'd been foolish. Angry with himself, Jordan shoved his hands deep into his pockets.

Jaywalking, he cut through the park and zigzagged down a couple of alleys to his air-conditioned office. He instantly felt better. Here he was king. Lord of his particular castle.

"Hey!" His daughter Hope offered him a wink and a smile that melted the ice around his heart. "You okay?"

"Why shouldn't I be?"

"I don't know, but you look—" she lifted a shoulder "—bugged, I guess would be the best word. Let me guess, you heard more gossip about the Kincaids."

She was teasing him, but he couldn't keep from saying, "I just had the pleasure of literally running into a couple of Larry's bastards."

Her shoulders sagged a bit. "You'd better get used to it, Dad. Whitehorn isn't exactly a metropolis."

"Yeah, yeah, I know." But it griped him just the same. "So, anything happening around here?"

"Not much, but what there was, I managed to handle," she said, needling a bit. "I am capable, you know."

"I know."

Hope paused, squared her shoulders and from her

desk chair looked her father steadily in the eye. "I hope you do, Dad. Sometimes I wonder."

"And why's that?" he asked, barely listening as he flipped through the envelopes on her desk.

"Because you don't seem to trust me."

Jordan's head snapped up. "It's not about trust, Hope. It's just that you're young and—"

"And not as tough as you think I should be," she filled in, sighing loudly. "Yeah, I know. The Baxter princess. Or heiress, or whatever it is you call me when you think I can't hear you."

"It just takes time." It was a phrase that rolled easily off his tongue, one he used whenever they had this particular discussion, which they seemed to be having a lot more often lately. Frowning he eyed the return address of one of the legal-size envelopes in his hand. "You know that."

"Yeah, yeah, 'Rome wasn't built in a day.' 'Patience is a virtue.' 'All good things come to those who wait.' 'With age comes reason.' I've heard 'em all before."

"Right," he said, moving toward the door to his office. His interest had been caught by the envelope he'd shuffled to the top of the stack.

He closed the door and ripped open the envelope. As he scanned the letter from a relative of George Sawyer's, the now-deceased lawyer who had drawn up the letter of intent from Jordan's uncle Cameron, Jordan Baxter started to smile. He rested a hip on the edge of his desk and felt a steady flow of elation run through his blood. At last there seemed to be some justice. The letter stated that while finally going through old papers that had sat in the attorney's basement for years, this relative had discovered a box of old legal documents, including the missing letter from Jordan's uncle, Cameron Baxter, willing Jordan the ranch and offering him the right of first refusal to any sale before Cameron's death.

Jordan's heart nearly stopped. He flipped over the page and saw the very document in question. Old and yellowed, smelling faintly of must, it stated all too clearly what Jordan had maintained for years.

His throat suddenly tightened as old emotions tore through him. Vividly he remembered his sixteenth birthday and his uncle Cameron promising him the Baxter place and handing him a copy of this very letter.

"Hot damn," he muttered, his mind spinning out possible legal scenarios as he tried to wrest the old place back from the Kincaids. In the end even his uncle had screwed him over, selling the place to the Kincaids and telling Jordan he'd never even given him the document. Since Jordan's only copy had burned in the fire that had taken his mother's life, he'd had no proof to the contrary.

"Stupid old bastard," he said, knowing that Cameron had somehow bribed George Sawyer to lie about the letter of intent, as well.

When Jordan had confronted his uncle about the sale of the property to the Kincaid family, Cameron had sighed heavily.

"What about the first right of refusal?" Jordan had demanded.

"I'm sorry, son," Cameron had said, placing a fatherly hand on Jordan's eighteen-year-old shoulders, "but I don't remember ever saying I'd give you first option." He'd spit a long stream of tobacco juice at the fence post near the old pump house. "'Sides, what could you do now, you're just a kid. I know how you feel about the place, but the plain fact of the matter is, I'm about broke. Got to sell."

Jordan had been thunderstruck. He'd swallowed hard, all his hopes and dreams sinking as fast as the lowering sun that had gilded the grassland and reflected in the windows of the old ranch house he loved.

"Tell you what I'll do," Cameron had said, "I'll see that some of the money ends up in your hands, to pay for college."

"No way. You promised. You signed a legal document."

For the first time he'd seen the vein throb beneath the brim of Cameron's dirty straw hat. "Then prove it," the other man had said. "Find the damned paper and take it to a judge."

"I will. I'll go to George Sweeney. If he's worth his salt, he's got a copy."

"I wouldn't count on it," Cameron had warned, and the hairs on the back of Jordan's neck had prickled in premonition. Sure as shootin', when he'd called the attorney late that night, George, not only Cameron's lawyer but his poker buddy as well, had claimed no knowledge of any paperwork concerning the ranch.

Jordan had been beaten.

Until now.

A cold smile twisted his lips. Nearly thirty years later, Jordan Baxter studied the yellowed, musty-smelling document with his uncle's signature scrawled across the bottom. His headache disappeared. Everything, it seemed, had changed when he'd ripped open this envelope. Justice and destiny had just met head-on.

He wasn't a scared, poor kid from the wrong side of the tracks any longer. At forty-six he was a millionaire many times over and a man to be reckoned with. The Kincaids were about to learn that lesson.

It was about time.

He reached for the phone and dialed his own attorney. Yep, the Kincaids's ship of fortune was just about to be turned into the wind. And Jordan Baxter was at the helm.

She was pregnant.

No question now, Gina thought as, seated on her bed in her room, she stared at the indicator strip. It was early morning, shafts of sunlight streamed through the open window, the sounds of the ranch filtered inside. Somewhere far off a rooster crowed, answered by a lark's song. Squirrels chattered, a lonely calf bawled and an engine rumbled to life.

A few minutes earlier she'd locked herself in the bathroom, taken the test and waited for the results.

They were most definitely positive.

Now what?

Flopping back onto the bed, she experienced a gamut of emotions. Elation, happiness, fear, joy, worry.

A mother! Gina Henderson, you're going to be a mother! Her heart pounded in anticipation and she couldn't stop a smile from toying with her lips.

The clock in the main hall struck seven, sending reverberating chords through the house. From the kitchen she heard the sound of voices and forced herself to her feet. With an odd mix of elation and dread, she regarded herself in the mirror mounted over her bureau. Twenty-seven and pregnant. That part sounded fine. Wait a minute, twenty-seven, pregnant and *unmarried*. There was the glitch.

Yet women had babies on their own all the time. Single mothers were a very viable part of society. Her hand rubbed the flat area of her abdomen. This wasn't the way she would have chosen to have a child. No, she'd always embraced the fantasy of husband who worked nine-to-five, a Cape Cod-style house surrounded by a white picket fence, a dog and cat… Oh, well. Her apartment in L.A. was large enough for her and the infant and she had some money saved, so she could take time off after the birth. Later she'd move and go back to work with Jack and—

And what about Trent?

She sighed, picked up a brush and absently ran it through her hair until it crackled. Surely he deserved to know about his child. Eventually. Once things had died down here at the ranch and all the Kincaid half brothers had settled. She'd go back to L.A., allow him time to get used to being part of this new piecemeal family and then, once she was through the first trimester of her pregnancy and the danger of miscarriage had diminished significantly, she'd call him with the happy news that he was about to become a father.

He had the right to know about the child; he didn't have the right to tell her what to do about it. She glanced out the open window and saw Mitch Fielding and Rand Harding in one of the paddocks with some of the steers milling in the early morning light. Garrett, with Brandon Harper in tow, joined them and they all four were quickly involved in a discussion. Laughter rippled upward in the clear morning air and somewhere nearby the dog let out a sharp bark.

The lace curtains billowed and she thought fleetingly that this ranch would be a perfect place to raise a child. In her mind's eye she saw a dark-haired boy racing through the fields, fishing in the creek, making forts in the hayloft, riding a spirited mustang on the deer trails that wove through the forested hills in the distance. Or maybe a cherub-faced girl with laughing blue eyes, wading and splashing in a favorite swimming hole, running in a field while trying to catch a butterfly, searching the creek for crayfish, learning to ride bareback with the help of her father…

Oh, God, quit this fantasizing right now! This isn't a scene from Little House on the Prairie, *for pity's sake!*

Her throat closed for a second and she felt the sting

of hot tears on the backs of her eyelids. From happiness? Or sorrow that the perfect little family she had envisioned for her child didn't exist? "Get over it," she growled, turning from the window. What she should do is call a local clinic, have another test done to verify, and tell Trent the truth. He had the right to know.

"Don't be a coward," she told herself, not even wanting to guess what Trent's reaction would be. Maybe he'd played this scenario half a dozen times with other women. She didn't think he had any children already as she'd delved pretty deeply into his past, known of half a dozen relationships he'd been involved in, but never thought he'd gone so far as to father a child.

Until now. With you.

Setting her brush on the bureau, she decided it would be best to hold her tongue. At least until she'd visited a doctor.

Tap, tap, tap.

Gina nearly jumped out of her skin. Trent! "Just a minute." She threw the contents of the pregnancy kit into a paper bag and stuffed it into the tiny trash basket in her room. She'd get rid of it later in town, so no one found it and asked embarrassing questions.

Oh, get over it, Gina, you're not fifteen, for crying out loud. No one should be going through your garbage, and even if they did, what you do is your business. Yours!

And Trent's!

Well, fine, that much is true, but this hide-and-seek, guilt-riddled routine is beneath you. Way beneath you!

She threw open the door and found herself staring straight into Blake Remmington's blue eyes. Relief flooded through her. Dressed in a casual sweater and slacks, he said, "Thought you might want an escort down to breakfast."

"Thoughtful of you," she said, surprised and warmed at his concern. "But you didn't have to. I could've found my way downstairs."

"I know. But I needed the company."

"In this houseful of half brothers?" she teased.

"Precisely my point."

Already the sound of rattling pans echoed through the corridors.

"Damn, I told Suzanne I'd help her this morning." She'd completely forgotten. From the minute she'd bought the pregnancy test, her mind had been wandering.

"Tomorrow's another day," he said without the hint of a smile.

"I could do the dishes or take care of lunch," she said as she walked out of her room.

"How long are you staying on?"

"Good question. I don't really know because I don't feel like I've really finished my job here, at least not until I find out if that seventh son really does exist."

"Still not sure?"

"Nope," she admitted with a sigh. "But I'd better figure it out soon and wrap it up. My brother is probably buried to his eyeballs in paperwork." *Jack, oh, God, what was she going to tell Jack?* Not that it was any of his business. As they reached the top of the stairs the scents of sizzling sausage and hot coffee rose to greet them. Gina's stomach quivered a bit and she mentally kicked herself. Just because she knew she was pregnant didn't mean that she had to buy into the morning sickness routine.

As they started down the stairs together, Blake spoke. "Besides, I thought you might want to talk about Trent."

"Why would I want to do that?" she asked as she glanced up at him.

He didn't bother to crack a smile. His jaw was as hard as granite, but he grabbed her hand. "That's what I was hoping you'd tell me."

It didn't take a brain surgeon to realize that he knew the truth. She'd bet her grandmother's diamond ring that Blake suspected she was pregnant. "I think maybe I'd better talk to Trent first," she said as they reached the bottom of the stairs.

"About what?" Trent's voice boomed from behind her.

Gina's heart nosedived as Trent stepped out of the living room, with Cade behind him. She didn't know how much of the conversation Trent had heard.

"What was it you wanted to talk to me about?" he said as Blake let go of her hand. Trent's gaze flicked to the movement; he hadn't missed it.

"I think I'll let you work this one out alone." Blake sent a silent message to Cade, who quickly picked up on it.

"Me, too." Cade nodded toward Blake. "Let me buy you a cup of coffee." They peeled off, heading in the direction of the kitchen where the sound of laughter floated down the hallways of the old house.

"Okay," Trent said, grabbing her elbow and tugging her into the living room where they were alone. "So, shoot, Gina." He folded his arms over his chest, blue eyes narrowed on her and a lock of dark hair fell over one eyebrow. Every muscle in his body was tense, his neck and shoulders stiff. "What is it you want to say to me?"

In for a penny, in for a pound. She swallowed hard, then forced her eyes to meet his. "I just found out this morning."

"What?"

Taking in a slow breath and silently praying for strength, she said, "The truth is that I'm pregnant, Trent. You're going to be a father."

Thirteen

"You're pregnant," Trent repeated, stunned.

Gina nodded and felt a deep sadness that he didn't wrap his arms around her, twirl her around and whoop. Clearing her throat, she watched the play of emotions on his face. "I just found out. I was suspicious, of course, but I finally did the test this morning and I thought I'd call a local clinic and double check."

"That…that would be a good idea," he said stiffly, and all at once Gina felt this gap between them, as if they were standing on separate sides of an unbridgeable abyss instead of on the faded rug in the living room of the Kincaid ranch.

"I thought you should know." Oh, God, why was this so difficult?

"After you told Blake." His lips compressed.

"Of course not. Blake just happened to see the pregnancy test in my sack from the pharmacy yesterday when I ran into you and several items dropped out. At least, that's how I think he knew—either that or he's psychic. Anyway, he put two and two together."

Trent didn't comment, just looked hard at her, as if searching for a lie somewhere in her story.

"Look, Trent, don't worry, when I get back to California, I'll—"

"Do what?" he said, and anger turned his face a nasty shade of red. His eyes glittered harshly. "You're going to have this baby, damn it."

"You bet I am," she flung back at him and stepped closer, bridging that gap between them. "I was saying that this is a big shock for me, too, and I'm not sure exactly how I'll handle it, but I'm going home, work until delivery, have the baby and eventually find a bigger apartment so I can raise my child."

"Our child."

"Yes."

"You're not going back to L.A."

"What?" She nearly laughed. "That's where I live, Trent."

"And what do you think you'll do there? Be a single mother?"

"I will be a single mother." Was the man dense?

Determination set his jaw. Blue eyes held hers and wouldn't let go. "If you're really pregnant—"

"I am. There's not much question about it," she said angrily.

"Well, you have been known to lie on more than one occasion. Especially to me."

"This is different."

"I'll say." Fury etched the edges of his mouth. "You should have told me earlier."

"I wasn't certain." She glared up at him. "I wasn't going to tell you and then have it turn out to be a false alarm." She threw one arm up in the air. "I don't know what you want me to do. I'd say I was sorry, but I'm not!"

"Good." He shoved stiff fingers through his hair. "We'll get married," he said out loud, as if she had no say in the matter whatsoever. "And...and you'll stay here."

"What?"

"You won't be going back to L.A."

"Are you out of your mind? Of course I'm going back to Los Angeles. In case you've forgotten, that's where I live!"

"Now wait a minute—"

"No, you wait a minute. Just because I'm pregnant doesn't mean you can bully me or boss me around." Anger spiked her words but deep inside she was hurt.

What did you expect? her mind taunted. *That he would be thrilled? That he would spin you off your feet, buy you dozens upon dozens of roses, get down on bended knee? Foolish, foolish woman.*

"I assume the baby's mine."

His words stung. Like salt poured into the open

wound of her heart. "Of course it's yours!" Oh, Lord, this wasn't going well, not well at all.

"Then it's pretty cut-and-dried, isn't it? We'll get married and the baby will have a name."

"Oh, no, what are you saying?" she whispered, shocked. What kind of marriage proposal was that?

"Admit it, Gina, this is what you've been angling for. I thought you were going to shake me down when I first met you and you lied about who you were, as if you didn't know me, then hopped in the sack with me and—"

She slapped him. Hard. "Don't you ever insinuate anything so vile again! Yes, it's true this baby was an accident, unplanned, but certainly not unwanted. I would think that considering your own personal situation, you might have a little more empathy." Tears burned the backs of her eyes, hot, bitter tears but not of shame. Oh, no, just demoralizing disappointment. "I— I didn't mean to hit you. I mean…I did, but I'm sorry." She lifted a hand, then let it fall. "I just hoped you'd understand."

His teeth ground together and a red welt appeared on his cheek. "That's the reason we're getting married."

"No way, Trent," she said, shaking her head. "I hate to sound cliché, but right now, I wouldn't marry you if you were the—"

"Last man on earth?" he said with a snort.

"The universe…and that includes the black holes, okay?"

"No, it's not okay. None of this is 'okay.'" He

walked to the window, stared outside and his rigid shoulders slumped. "So just deep-six the theatrics, Gina, or Celia, or whoever the hell you really are. We have a problem and—"

"Correction." Striding up to him, she poked a finger hard against his chest and swallowed against the tears of frustration lodging in her throat. A breeze slipped through the window, toying with Trent's hair, caressing her hot cheeks. "We have a baby," she said, her voice lower than normal. "It's not a problem. At least, it's not for me."

"The solution is to get married."

"Are you out of your mind? Have you heard a word of our conversation?" It was her turn to be flabbergasted. She held both of her hands near her head, palms out, as if surrendering. But she wasn't. "I think we should both slow down a minute here, okay? Marriage? You're talking *marriage?* Oh, come on. We don't even know each other well enough…we can't get married, I mean…think about it, Trent, you live in Texas and I'm in L.A. I have a job—no, make that a career to consider."

He winced when she mentioned her work. "I'll take care of you."

"You'll 'take care of me'? Oh, God, don't even suggest anything so remotely archaic, okay?" Her head was spinning, her pride wounded to the core, her pain deep-seated. She placed a hand over her abdomen, as if she were protecting her child because Trent's reaction was all wrong. All wrong. "I'm not some frail little insecure woman, you know, no hothouse flower who can't stand on her own two feet, a woman who doesn't feel complete without a man. No way. I'm not going to marry someone out of some sense of duty." Her temper inched skyward. She longed to hear him tell her he loved her, that he wanted to spend the rest of his life with her, that together the three of them would become a close-knit family, the kind neither she nor Trent had ever experienced. But this, this pathetic reasoning, wasn't even a proposal.

Worse, he thought she'd tried to shake him down, to blackmail him into this. What a joke, a horrible, horrible joke.

"The baby needs two parents." He was adamant when he turned his eyes back to look at her, some of his anger appeared to be replaced with concern.

"Two parents who love him and each other," she agreed, glaring at him, her heart aching as she bared her soul. "Two people who want him." Again she pressed on her stomach. "Not a couple of people who throw in together because the innocent child just happens to be coming along. No way."

"Listen to me, Gina. This is my child, too." He grabbed her then, his steely fingers wrapping around her arm. Beneath the anger in his eyes she saw deeper emotions and a pain she didn't begin to understand. "Like it or not, I have a say in it." Grooves deepened at the edges of his mouth and his eyebrows slammed together. "So what're you holding out for? Money? Is that it?"

She gasped. "Is that what you think?" Disappointment burrowed deep in her soul, gnawed at her heart.

"As I said, I felt this was some kind of shakedown from the beginning."

She nearly slapped him again. Instead she yanked her arm away and felt the weight of disappointment heavy on her shoulders. "With you it's always about money, isn't it?" she whispered sadly, then steeled herself, straightening her spine and tossing her hair from her eyes. "Well, it isn't for me. Believe it or not, it never has been. If I'd been interested in 'shaking you down,' I would have found a better way to do it, believe me. Now, listen, I've said all I have to say. I've got a job to do here and I intend to do it, after which I'm going back to California."

"Just like that?"

"You bet. And as for you, don't you have some oil wells that need drilling somewhere? You know, like Texas or Wyoming, or the Yukon? I hear they're finding gushers in Siberia. Maybe you should go and check it out." With that, she turned on a heel and stalked down the hall, anger radiating from her in furious, hot waves.

How could he be so callous? And how could she care for a man who thought she was capable of such dirty, underhanded, vile— "Stop it," she ordered herself. There was no reason to dwell on any of his motivations. Maybe he was just in shock. But it didn't matter.

She could take care of herself. And a baby.

In fact, she'd make a helluva mother and probably a

halfway decent dad. At that thought her heart twisted, but she told herself that her once-idyllic Norman Rockwell envisionment of her life and marriage would have to be adjusted.

She was going to become a mother.

Rubbing his stinging cheek, Trent watched her march off in a tornado of self-righteous ire. His thoughts were going in a thousand directions all at once. A baby? What would he do with a baby? What would he do without one? The kid wasn't even here yet and he felt this swelling sense of propriety and something else, way beyond pride, a newfound fear for the unborn child. Now, Trent was vulnerable.

And he'd made a mess of things with Gina, but she'd blindsided him. He walked out of the living room and upstairs, then paused at the doorway to her bedroom. He looked inside to the mussed bed where she'd slept. The scent of her perfume still hung in the air. Was it his imagination or did that one room seem to have more sunshine than any other part of the house? Why did her off-key singing amuse rather than irritate him? What was it about her that made her sexy without a drop of makeup or a comb through her hair?

Hell, he had it bad. Blake, damn him, was right. Trent couldn't get Gina out of his mind. He walked to his room and picked up his wallet and keys. Stuffing them into his pocket, he started down the stairs.

How could he possibly be a father? What did he

know about parenting? Larry Kincaid, his biological sire, had been worse than a cad, a man he'd never known, a gambler, cheat, womanizer who had kids and never bothered to even meet them. No, Trent thought angrily, he wouldn't make the same mistakes—be as distant and uncaring as that bastard had been. Nor would he be a dishrag the likes of Harold Remmington. That guy…well, he'd been little better than Larry.

But Garrett… Trent imagined the older man had been a helluva dad even though his own son, Larry, had ended up a mess. Trent didn't have a clue as to how Garrett's daughter, Alice, had turned out. No matter, it wasn't because Garrett hadn't been in there pitching, doing the best he could, spending his life trying to be the best damned father in the world.

Trent knew it instinctively.

On the landing, he paused as the reality of the situation hit him with the force of a fist to his chest. Gina was pregnant. With his kid. His throat tightened. Memories of another time and place washed over him in painful ripples as he thought about Beverly, haughty and beautiful, telling him he was going to be a father. For such a short time he'd been buoyed with new, exciting feelings of paternity. Elated, he'd imagined his son's or daughter's birth, toddling years and elementary school highs and lows, but his bubble had been burst, pricked by the evil, lying tongue of a woman he'd never loved.

But this time was different.

He'd make sure of it.

Trent took one step toward the kitchen, then stopped himself. It wasn't just because of the baby that he was feeling this way, he realized. It was because of Gina. Like it or not, he was falling in love with her and he had been since the first time he'd laid eyes on her nearly two months earlier.

He'd just been kidding himself.

The tension in the room was so thick you could cut it with a butter knife, Garrett thought as he finished his stack of waffles and carried his plate to the sink. He, Gina, and Larry's sons had crowded around the kitchen table and discussed the operations of the ranch. Garrett had explained that each of the heirs would own a portion of the spread, but some might want to be silent partners. Others would want to be a part of the day-to-day operations.

Cade had assured Garrett that he would stay on, and Mitch had agreed to work on the spread, as well. Brandon hadn't committed as yet, nor had Adam, who seemed edgy and anxious to leave. Probably had some unsuspecting corporation to gut, Garrett thought unkindly. Adam was the one who could really use this place to get in touch with his heart, but then, it was Adam's decision.

Garrett handed his empty plate to Suzanne, who was loading the dishwasher, then refilled his coffee cup. He took a sip and walked back to the table where his grandsons were beginning to disperse. Blake had been quieter than usual, as if something was bothering him, yet he'd decided to stay on at the ranch, at least for a while.

Trent had been downright silent for most of the meal. If he'd decided how involved he wanted to be here in Whitehorn, he was keeping it to himself. He'd been more intense than usual, brooding in a dark way. He'd cast a few looks in Gina's direction and she'd met his gaze coldly.

Lover's spat, Garrett guessed.

Gina, usually fresh-faced and smiling, hadn't been herself these past few days. This morning was the worst. She'd barely eaten, jumped up and offered to help Suzanne with the dishes, and generally been preoccupied for the past hour.

Probably because of Trent.

The unspoken words hanging between those two had been as cold as the Ice Age.

Garrett had hoped that whatever was between them would have eased off a mite, but it seemed as if just the opposite were true. If anything, they were more bristly with each other than ever.

Something was going on.

And he was damned sure he wouldn't like it. He finished his coffee and set his cup in the sink. Cade and Mitch followed suit; they were two who weren't interested in sitting around the table. Adam had agreed to look over the property, but Garrett was afraid Larry's firstborn was only going to eye it to see how much it was worth.

"Guess I'd better mosey out and check on the stock," Garrett said to Suzanne. "Rand's probably already waiting on me."

"Well, don't keep him. He's supposed to be fitted for a tuxedo today. He's part of Leanne's wedding party, you know."

At the mention of a wedding, Gina's back stiffened. Quickly she untied her apron.

"How's Rand taking it that his baby sister's getting hitched?" Garrett asked Suzanne.

She laughed. "I think he's relieved. And Bill's a great guy. Rand's best friend."

"Then he should be pleased," Garrett said. "I'll see that he makes the fitting." Garrett reached for his hat and noticed that Trent's face muscles had tightened and Gina's skin had blanched a bit at the talk of the upcoming wedding.

What the hell was going on? As far as he could see, they didn't even know the people involved. "Oh, by the way, I've found someone to take on the chores around here," he said to Suzanne. "I'll let you know when she can start. She's a real nice gal with a baby of her own."

"Great," Suzanne said as she turned back to the dishes. "Not that I don't love working here from dawn until dusk," she teased.

Trent downed his coffee, glanced at Gina, then, expression grim as all get-out, said to the room at large, "I'll be in the den. I've got some calls to make." Without another word, he stormed out of the kitchen, his boot heels ringing down the hallway.

"I wonder what's got into him," Suzanne remarked,

and Gina bit her lip as she hung her apron on a hook near the back door.

"Bad mood," Blake observed.

"The worst." Gina wiped her hands on a nearby towel. "I think I'll run into town for a while. I'll be back this afternoon." She forced a smile that didn't quite fit her face, then hurried upstairs. A few minutes later, lugging her purse, she raced out the front door. It slammed behind her.

"Talk about bad moods," Suzanne observed. "It seems infectious."

"That it does," Garrett said, watching through the window as Gina jogged to her Explorer, climbed inside, then roared off down the dirt lane. "Do you know what's going on?" Garrett asked Blake.

"Nope." But the man was a bad liar. He knew something, he just wasn't saying. Avoiding his grandfather's eyes, Blake shoved out his chair and stretched. "I imagine Trent and Gina will figure it out."

"What's 'it'?"

Blake lifted a shoulder.

The phone rang once before Garrett could reach for the kitchen extension; he heard Trent pick up in the den.

"I guess I'd better see about the yearlings in the north pasture," he decided, still bothered about the simmering unspoken battle that he'd just witnessed. "If you're interested, Blake, why don't you come along?"

"I just might."

Garrett stepped onto the porch and started pulling on

his boots. He heard a commotion through the screen door and looked up just as Trent shoved it open.

"Jordan Baxter's on the telephone," Trent said, his face muscles stretched tight as tanned leather as his eyes scanned the parking lot. When he saw that Gina's truck was missing, he frowned. He swung his gaze back to Garrett. "Baxter wants to talk to you."

The warning hairs on the back of Garrett's neck raised one by one. He pulled on the second boot and slowly stood, his knees popping a little and the arthritis that sometimes flared in his shoulder beginning to ache. "Somehow I have a feeling this isn't going to be good news."

Fingers tight around the steering wheel, Gina drove on automatic pilot toward town. Images of Trent darted through her mind. She saw him in a business suit, smiling seductively, or in bed, naked, his skin taut, his muscles flexing as he made love to her, or in jeans and a sweatshirt, surveying the Kincaid ranch. Her throat tightened and she battled tears again.

"It's just hormones." She tried to convince herself, dashing the horrid drops from her eyes and sniffing loudly. She had to quit thinking about him. About what could have been.

"Ha!"

He'd proposed, hadn't he?

Done his duty.

Angrily, she took a turn a little too sharply, then

eased off on the accelerator. She had a baby to worry about. She couldn't afford to be careless. Never again.

On a whim, she veered east on Highway 17, deciding to visit Winona Cobbs's secondhand store.

The gates were wide open as Gina drove into the dusty lot where junk from the turn of the twentieth century to the millennium had collected around a trailer Winona called home. Ancient, disemboweled cars filled one corner while another was chock-full of used farm equipment. Sheds offered up more personal merchandise, everything from treadle sewing machines to plumbing fixtures to secondhand clothes and shoes.

But Winona wasn't anywhere on the lot. Gina climbed out of her car and walked up the steps of the trailer and knocked on the door. "Ms. Cobbs?" she called loudly, pounding with her fist, hoping to get the woman's attention. "Are you home? Ms. Cobbs?" But no one answered and there wasn't any life in the yard, aside from the honey bees that buzzed around several hives tucked near the fence in one corner of the property.

The psychic apparently didn't believe that anyone would stop by and rip her off.

There was no reason to stay and wait. Winona might be gone for hours, so Gina slid behind the wheel of the Explorer again, tipped a pair of sunglasses onto the bridge of her nose and tried to concentrate on Larry's seventh illegitimate son. She switched on the radio and drove off in a cloud of dust, but her mind kept straying from Larry's baby to the baby she herself had on the way.

Despite a bank of clouds gathering in the western sky, Gina felt her bad mood lighten. She was going to have a baby!

She smiled at the thought of becoming a mother and though Trent's reaction still stung, she hummed along with a Faith Hill song and drove into the town of White-horn, a small speck on the map that was becoming more and more familiar to her.

She spied people she'd met walking along the side-walks or driving by in pickups and cars. She'd learned the back streets and alleys of the town nearly as well as some of the locals. At a stoplight she waited for a couple to cross the street and her heart twisted. A man and woman walked in front of her Explorer, their hands linked. The woman carried her purse and a diaper bag, the man, most likely her husband, was fitted with a front pack wherein a tiny baby, only a few blond curls visible, was resting.

Tears sprang to Gina's eyes and she quickly dashed them away, clearing her throat and reminding herself that she would love her baby enough for two parents. She didn't need a husband. And she didn't need Trent. She still winced when she thought that he'd seen her pregnancy as a way to squeeze money out of him.

A horn blasted behind her and she realized the crosswalk was clear. Jittery, she pulled up to the Hip Hop and spied not only Lily Mae in her usual booth, but Winona Cobbs seated in a booth near the counter and perusing a paper.

Sniffing back the last hint of any maudlin tears, Gina parked and hurried inside. A bell jingled as the door opened and she was greeted with the smells of coffee, donuts, and frying bacon.

The booths were nearly full, the midmorning crowd hovering over java, pastries and conversation.

Gina didn't waste any time. She walked boldly up to Winona's booth and asked, "Mind if I join you?"

"Not at all." The short, round woman tucked the crossword puzzle she'd been working on into an oversize bag. "Sit," she said, waving to the bench on the other side of the booth. Her bracelets jangled and her bright eyes seemed to pierce straight to Gina's soul. "You're worried about something?"

"A million things," Gina admitted, ordering a glass of iced tea from Emma. "But the reason I wanted to talk to you is because the rumor around town is that you're psychic."

Winona nodded. "I have the gift."

"Then, I was hoping you could help me. I told you before that I think that Larry Kincaid fathered a seventh baby—and I haven't been able to locate him." She reached into her purse and pulled out Larry Kincaid's journal, with the pages open to the notation about the seventh son. She slid it across the table to the older woman. Winona adjusted her shawl and fingered the open page. Closing her eyes, she concentrated, deep grooves etching her forehead. "This is not a fake. You're concerned that it was a notation made after some woman called, a woman with a vendetta intent upon Larry Kincaid, but there is a child, a boy child. The information is correct, but…" Her lips drew hard, her eyebrows pinched together. "But I cannot see how he found out, or who is the mother of the baby."

Winona shook her head, the silvering braid wrapped around her head moving slowly side to side. "The woman who bore Larry's last child prefers to be anonymous."

Gina's heart sank.

"The only sense I get is that the mother is nearby. Somewhere here in Montana. But she is very worried. Not unhappy." Winona opened her eyes and stared at Gina long and hard. "The boy is the light of her life. Just as your child will be yours."

Gina nearly choked on a swallow of coffee. How had Winona Cobbs known that she was pregnant?

The door to the café opened and Christina Montgomery flew into the shop. She took a corner booth and picked up a menu. She looked pale and seemed upset, her blue eyes shadowed.

Winona sighed and her lips folded in upon themselves. "What's wrong?"

The older woman's expression turned concerned. "I'd have to say that the water here in Whitehorn must be increasing the chances of fertility."

"Now, wait a minute…"

But Winona's eyes were focused on the girl slumped disconsolately at the booth. Christina ordered a soda and stared out the window, her manicured fingers drumming an anxious tattoo on the table.

"She's got the glow, too."

"What glow?" Gina asked. The girl was far from glowing. If anything, her mood was somber and dark.

"A pregnant glow. It's in her aura."

"And you can see it?" Gina asked, unable to hide her skepticism. Though she often ran with her hunches in an investigation, they were usually based on scientific evidence and fact.

Yes, but didn't you, too, come seeking counsel from the psychic? When all else fails...

"Certainly I can see it. Not only in her, but in you, as well."

Gina could barely believe her ears.

"But in Christina's case there's a mist of unhappiness surrounding her."

"'A mist of unhappiness'?" Was this for real?

"Uh-huh." Winona's eyes slitted and for a few seconds Gina had the eerie feeling that the owner of the junkyard was actually reading Christina's mind. But that was crazy. "It has to do with the father, but I can't tell who he is." Winona rubbed the crystal pendant at her neck with calloused fingers. "Oh, there is going to be trouble. Serious trouble. Nothing good is going to come of this."

"How do you know?" Gina asked, and in an instant the older woman turned her eyes away from Christina. Once again they were warm and a smile curved over her uncolored lips.

"I don't know how. As I said, it's a gift."

"Or a curse."

"Depends upon how you look at it. As for Christina, unfortunately I only see pain in her future, but you're a different story."

Gina couldn't help rising to the bait. "I am. How so?"

"It's simple." Winona picked up her cup of coffee and held it to her lips. "In your case you love the man who is the father of your child."

Gina bit her tongue against the argument that leaped to her lips. Because it was true, damn it, she did love Trent. Foolish as it was. "That doesn't mean I don't have my share of problems."

"None that can't be overcome," Winona said sagely as she took a sip of coffee then set down her cup. To Gina's surprise she reached across the table and took Gina's hand in hers. "What you don't understand is that the father of your baby loves you very much."

"No, I don't think—"

"And therein lies the problem. You're not thinking the right way—with faith rather than mistrust. Listen to me, Gina. Whether you believe it or not, the truth is that Trent Remmington, the father of the child you carry, loves you with all his heart and soul."

"You know this?" Gina couldn't believe it. It was too far-fetched.

"And that's not all. You love him, but pride won't allow you to admit it."

Fourteen

"You goin' somewhere?" Blake asked as he watched Trent stuff all his belongings into his duffel bag.

"I'll be back," Trent said with determination. He glanced around the tiny room he'd called home since landing in Montana, searching for anything he'd need. "You can count on it." He yanked the zipper closed.

"When?"

He met his brother's curious gaze. "As soon as I can."

"Where are you going?"

Trent didn't have time for explanations. He wanted to take care of business, clear his head and return on the first flight he could find. But he had a business to run, and his life to bring into order. "I've got to leave for Houston, A.S.A.P. I just got a call from one of my foremen. There's all sorts of garbage goin' on in the company and it needs my personal attention."

"Such as?"

"Such as talk of a strike, for starters. And that's not the half of it. I've got a couple of wells that'll be shut down in Wyoming and I've got to handle it." His gaze clashed with eyes identical to his own. "I don't know where I'll land or when."

"Sure that's the reason you're takin' off?"

"What're you getting at?" Trent said, bristling.

"Looks to me like you might be running away," Blake accused. "Just like our old man."

Trent hiked the strap of his bag onto his shoulder. Not for the first time would he have loved to knock his smug brother down a peg, but though his fist actually flexed, he slowly uncurled it. This wasn't the time to round on his twin and knock him from here to eternity.

"You don't know what you're talking about."

"I know you're running out on Gina. On the baby."

"Like hell." Trent resisted arguing any further. "I'll call her later."

"Should I give her the message?"

Trent's back teeth ground together. He dropped his bag, turned to face his brother again and said, "Don't say anything, all right? The best thing for you to do is to stay out of this."

"You know, you're taking a chance. She might not wait for you."

"I said, butt out."

"I wish I could. But you're my brother. The only one who's full-blooded. The only one I grew up with. I care what happens to you. To Gina and the baby."

Trent hesitated, felt a damned lump fill his throat. This was not the time to lose focus. "I can take care of myself and I'll deal with Gina on my own terms," Trent said.

"Always the loner."

"Always." But it was a lie. Now there was Gina. And the baby. And the fact was that he had to leave Montana to straighten some things out before he returned. For good. To claim his wife and child, for like it or not, he was going to convince Gina to marry him. But not yet. There were a few ducks that needed to be put in order. He started with Blake. "Look, if you feel the need to bond with a brother or two, I think you can take your pick. Larry left quite an assortment to choose from."

"Right. I choose you."

Trent stopped short. The honesty in his brother's eyes, the pain they'd shared together, was all too visible. His throat caught. He swallowed hard. His voice, when he found it, was raspy. "Find someone else, Blake." With that he grabbed his bag, stopped in the den and snapped his laptop into its case then stormed out of the house. Blake's words echoed in his mind. *You know, you're taking a chance. She might not wait for you...*

He spied Garrett and the old dog near the machine shed. Figuring he'd better take the time to tell the old man that he had to leave for business but that he'd call, he crossed the parking lot and leaned against the fence.

As he said his goodbyes, the accusations in Garrett's eyes mirrored those he'd seen in Blake's.

"What about Gina?"

"She was gone when I got the call. I'll phone her later."

"Do that." It was an order. Not a suggestion.

"I will."

"And take my advice," Garrett said, propping up the brim of his Stetson with his thumb. "Slow down enough to enjoy life. It's over sooner than any of us like to think."

"I'll remember that," Trent said. He was already re-thinking his priorities. He rubbed his cheek where Gina had struck it and knew he'd find a way to make amends.

"Do." Garrett whistled to the dog and strode off.

Trent turned on his heel and strode to his rental car. Ever since Gina had told him he was going to be a father, he saw the world a little differently. He threw his bag into the back seat of the car. Behind the wheel, he fired the engine and took off, spraying gravel as he followed the rutted lane toward the main road. Through the passenger window he saw a horse, a lone stallion, head raised, nostrils to the wind, far apart from the rest of the herd. Trent's eyes narrowed on the white stallion for just a second and the animal swung his great head in his direction, ears pricked forward, then reared as the car raced past. The horse was a loner. A rogue. A maverick.

Just like me.

Barely slowing as he entered the main road, Trent shook the image of the stallion from his mind and gripped the wheel with tense fingers. In the past few weeks his entire life had been ripped to shreds, everything he'd believed in destroyed. He had a new family, if only he would embrace it; he had a woman he loved, if only he could convince her of that fact; and he had a baby on the way.

This was his chance. If he hadn't blown it already by not waiting for her. But he didn't turn around. He didn't have time because all of a sudden his entire life was looming ahead of him and he was anxious to get on with it. Right now, he had business to attend to, important business. But first on the agenda when the plane touched down in Houston was to visit the jewelry store and pick out a ring with the biggest damned diamond he could find.

When he returned to Whitehorn, he'd find a way to convince Gina that he loved her. If he had to, he'd spend the rest of his life proving it.

Gina tried to shake off the malaise that seemed to cling to her like a shroud. So she was pregnant, so she was alone, so Trent had been gone from the ranch for more than two days without any word from him. So what? She sat on the back porch swing, her laptop beeping that its battery was about to die, and slowly rocked. She looked across the windswept acres and watched the cattle lumber through the dry fields.

She was no closer to finding Larry's last heir than she had been when she'd landed on the ranch over two weeks earlier. Jack was making noise about her return-

ing and though she hated to leave, the truth of the matter
was that she was spinning her wheels here. Sooner or
later she had to return to Southern California to face the
music. Jack deserved to know the truth.

Inside she heard the men collecting. Trent, Adam
and Brandon had left, at least temporarily, but Mitch,
Cade and Blake had stayed on. Along with Rand and
Garrett, they were milling in the living room, waiting
for Wayne Kincaid to arrive to discuss legalities concerning the land. From what she could gather, Jordan
Baxter was determined to stir up trouble for the
Kincaids, making a claim that he had some kind of right
to the land. Then there was the press.

For the past few days the phone had been ringing
off the hook, local reporters interested in writing
about Larry's sons, all six of them. So far, Gina had
avoided being interviewed. If she stayed here much
longer, though, she'd have to give some quotes. She'd
thought about this and it wasn't necessarily a bad
idea. If she admitted she was looking for Larry's
seventh son, perhaps someone who knew something
about that damned notation in Larry's journal might
just come forward.

Her computer beeped again and she snapped it off.
She needed to get away from the house, to consider the
rest of her life, to find a way to control the ache in her
heart whenever she thought about Trent.

She'd returned to the ranch to find him gone—his
things packed, his room empty. Blake had tried to

reassure her that Trent would return, he'd call, he'd contact her, but she was certain it was a lie.

She walked up the stairs and changed into a pair of jeans and T-shirt. It was true Trent had asked her to marry him, but it had been a reaction, the "right thing" to do. Obviously he'd had a change of heart and taken her rejection at face value. "So what did you expect?" she asked herself as she pulled her hair back into a ponytail and eyed her reflection in the cracked mirror. "Hearts and flowers? Love letters and diamonds? A tortured admission that he couldn't live without you?" She frowned at the woman in the mirror, the woman whose green eyes looked ready to fill with tears. "Get real, Gina. You know better."

But you love him! Face it. You should have accepted his marriage proposal when he offered it. It would have been best for you, best for the baby.

"And it would have been trapping him. No thank you."

She snapped the rubber band in place and took the stairs to the first floor. The men were deep in conversation in the living room and she made her way through the kitchen and out the back door. Needing fresh air and time to herself, she saddled her favorite mare and rode away from the center of the ranch.

"Let's go," she said, clucking to the palomino. With a burst of energy, the horse stretched out, strides lengthening, the wind rushing against Gina's face and cheeks. Tears blurred her eyes and she let them flow, telling herself it was from the fresh mountain air, not because her heart was breaking.

"Run, damn you, run," she said, leaning over the game little mare's shoulders, and feeling the slap of the mane against her chin. Upward, through the trees, along the trail she rode as sunlight and shadows speckled the ground. A jackrabbit hopped across the path, diving into the brambles as they passed.

Gina's heart pounded and she thought of Trent. God, how she loved him, more than was respectable, more than any sane woman should care for a man. Gina, the woman who had vowed to never let a man close to her, to never trust someone who wasn't steadfast, true and dedicated. She'd been looking for the boy next door, a man she could depend on, not a self-serving man like the father who had left her mother with two children to raise. And then she'd foolishly fallen for a maverick oilman, a loner, a rogue who lived his life his own way.

A lump formed in her throat and she steadfastly swallowed it back. Well, it did no good to wallow or cry over a man like Trent Remmington. No, she'd just have to make it on her own. She'd managed to take care of herself up to now; she was certain she could be both mother and father to her child.

The trees gave way to the meadow where she and Trent had nearly made love over a week earlier. Her heart wrenched and again the tears started to flow. Two pheasants flew across the mare's path. Wings whirred, feathers swirled. The horse broke stride and stumbled. Gina pitched forward. Her heart flew to her throat.

She held on to the reins.

Spooked, the mare reared and Gina was thrown back. Then the palomino, as if branded by hot iron, shot forward. "No!" The creek loomed closer. Hoof beats thundered in her eardrums.

Oh, God, no! Gina tried to right herself, but couldn't. She scrabbled for the saddle horn, her head hanging down near the horse's shoulder, her ponytail touching the ground, her right foot caught in the stirrup.

"Whoa!" she cried. "Stop, oh, please—"

She felt the mare's muscles bunch, heard the rush of water.

"Please…no!" The horse sprang, beneath her the creek roared, swift water splashing and tumbling over stones as it cut downhill. The saddle shifted and Gina screamed. Hooves hit the far bank, then scrambled. Dust flew. Her head hit the dirt. Pain ripped up from Gina's hip and exploded in her brain. She screamed and her foot slipped out of her boot.

Thud! She hit the ground hard, every bone rattling in her body. Pain ricocheted up her spine. For a second she was conscious, the darkening sky swirling above her, the ground tilting. She felt something deep within her rend…a warm wetness slide down her jeans.

The baby! Oh, please God, not the baby! Anything else, but please, please, keep this precious baby alive…

Somewhere she heard the sound of a horse neighing and the barking of a dog, and then as she struggled to find her feet, she felt the warm comfort of darkness seduce her, the blackness at the corners of her vision closing in. Then with a sigh and a profound sadness over her loss, she let out a plaintive moan, wrapped her arms around her body and fell back onto the cushion of grass.

"What do you mean, she's not here?" Trent demanded when Garrett gave him the news that Gina wasn't in the ranch house. Hot, tired, and out of sorts from a whirlwind trip, he'd barely gotten out of the rental car when he'd spied Garrett eyeing the workmen assembling the indoor arena.

"She went off riding earlier this afternoon and hasn't come back yet." Garrett ran a gloved hand along the corner of a two-by-four.

"What time was that?"

"Four, maybe five hours ago." Garrett was chewing on a blade of dry grass. Studying Trent, he shifted the blade from one side of his mouth to the other. "I'm a little worried since she didn't come back for dinner, but I figure she's had a lot on her mind and needs some time alone." His blue eyes were flatly assessing. "I figure she'll be back soon."

Trent wasn't in the mood to wait. He'd done enough of that in the past couple of days. And the times he'd tried to call the ranch all of the lines had been busy with his half brothers either on the phone or the Internet. "I think I'll go looking for her. If I miss her and if she shows up back here, don't let her go anywhere."

"You think I could stop her?"

"You could damn well try." Trent wasn't in the mood

for nonsense. He'd spent the better part of the past forty-eight hours kicking himself up one side and down the other for being such a fool. He'd slept maybe three hours in total and was in one bear of a mood, but the ring in his pocket eased his mind. Wherever he found Gina, he was going to tell her how much she meant to him, that pregnant or not, he wanted her for his wife, that he couldn't bear to think of a future without her.

He saddled the roan gelding he'd claimed for his use and took off through the hills. Dusk was lengthening the shadows of the surrounding trees and the sky had taken on a lavender hue.

In his peripheral vision Trent spied the lone white stallion, the solitary horse he'd thought was so like himself. "Not anymore," he vowed as his gelding stretched out, eating up the ground, racing as if against the wind.

"Hey!" He heard Blake's voice and looked over his shoulder. His brother was jogging out of the ranch house and had stopped to talk to Garrett. Another fence he had to mend, Trent thought with a scowl. He saw Blake start for the stables, then turned his attention to the hills. Yep, this place wouldn't be a bad spot to raise a family and it was a middle ground, not Texas and surely not Southern California. Both he and Gina could work from here, take life a little slower and watch their child grow. At the thought of the baby, Trent's chest swelled.

He might not have had exemplary male role models in his life, but there was no reason to think he couldn't be a damned good father. The best. He urged the roan into the woods and up the familiar trail that wound through the pines to the meadow where he and Gina had nearly made love. For a reason he couldn't fathom he felt she was there, and the need to see her again, to touch her, to hold her, to promise to love her for all eternity, pounded through his blood.

"Come on, come on," he said urgently, suddenly anxious to find her. The trees gave way and he spied the horse. A smile broke out on his lips and he nearly laughed until he realized the saddle was askew, twisted around the mare's belly.

His gut twisted.

Where was Gina?

He kicked the gelding, spurred him into the field, and his eyes swept the hillside where sunlight was fading fast and the first stars of twilight were beginning to glow.

Then he saw her. Crumpled on the grass, blood at her head, her skin a pasty white. His heart froze, but he kicked the roan and rode like a bat out of hell, jumping down from the saddle before the horse had time to stop.

"Gina! Oh, God, Gina!" Rushing to her side, his blood thundering through his head, he dropped to his knees. "Gina, oh, love…please, please…" His throat tightened and he tried to think. She was breathing, her pulse still strong. The wound on her head was shallow, the blood beginning to crust.

"Gina, can you hear me?" he whispered, his arms surrounding her. "Oh, baby, hang on. I'll take care of you."

"W-what?" Her eyelids fluttered open and eyes as green as a spring meadow stared into his. "Trent?"

"Shh." Tears filled his eyes. "You'll be all right. I'll get help."

"W-what happened?" she asked, wincing as she moved.

"Stay still. Shh." He pressed his lips to her dirt-smudged and bloody forehead. "You'll be fine."

"But…" She struggled with a memory and then he saw the fear slash through her eyes. "The baby…"

"Will be fine."

"I don't know…I don't think…" And then she was gone again, her eyes closing as he held her to him and noticed the stain on her jeans, the dark red splash that marred the denim.

"It'll be all right," he promised. *And if we can't save this one, we'll have others. A dozen if you want.*
He lifted her into his arms and gently carried her toward his horse. Somehow he'd get her down the hillside and he'd do it quick if he had to carry her every step of the way himself.

"Trent!" Blake's voice rang across the hills and he looked up to find his brother astride the damned white stallion. He was off the horse in an instant. "What happened?"

"I don't know."

"Lay her down so I can examine her and go get help," Blake ordered.

"I can't leave her."

"Like hell, Trent. I'm the doctor, remember. Now go

on and get help. She needs to get to a hospital. See if they've got life flight or something."

Trent was astride his horse and racing down the hillside at a dead gallop. His blood ran cold in his veins and his teeth ground together in a jaw tense with determination. He wasn't going to lose Gina now, not when he'd finally found her.

There were voices…so many voices… Gina awoke in the hospital, on a narrow bed covered with soft green sheets. Her head felt as if it had been cracked open and her entire body ached. She winced against the fluorescent light and expected to find a doctor examining her. Instead she found herself staring directly into Trent Remmington's worried eyes.

He blinked against a sheen of tears and managed a smile. "I knew you'd make it," he said, though the crack in his voice belied his words. "You're just too tough to let go that easy."

"Am I?" She felt anything but tough at this moment in time.

"Where am I?"

"The Whitehorn Memorial Hospital."

But there was something wrong, something more, a heaviness and sense of doom she carried in her heart. Then she remembered. "The…the baby?"

"Is fine," Trent assured her. "But I'm not certain about the kid's father. He nearly fell into a million pieces." His throat worked and she felt the sting of tears when she saw the love and raw pain in his eyes. "Everything's going to be fine," he said gruffly. "The doctor said you should make it to term…well, if you follow his instructions."

"I will," she vowed, relieved.

"Good." Trent took her hand in his, frowned at the sight of the IV buried in the back of her wrist. "He also said the best thing for you to do is to marry me."

"What?" she said, then realized it was a joke. "The man must have brutal sense of humor."

Trent winced visibly. "Look, I know what you think about me, and believe me, I understand, but I'd already decided I loved you, needed you and wanted you and… Oh, hell—" he swallowed hard and looked her straight in the eye "—that I couldn't live without you. I went to Houston to straighten things out at the company and—"

"Shh." Blinding pain cut through her heart. "You don't have to do this. Or say anything. Just because I had an accident and nearly lost the baby doesn't mean you're obligated or—oh!" She gasped as his lips crashed down on hers and he kissed the very breath from her lungs.

When he lifted his head, tears sheened his eyes. "I *want* to marry you, damn it. Do you hear me. I *want* to be your husband and the baby's father and even… God, even if you'd lost him, I'd still want you to live with me for the rest of my life."

She wanted to believe him, ached to trust his words, and the raw emotion twisting his features nearly convinced her.

"I'll do whatever it takes," he said, his voice ragged, his soul bare. "You can work. We can live in L.A. Whatever, but I'd like to start out here. Just you and me…and then when the baby comes, the three of us." The fingers over her hand tightened. "I love you, Gina. That's the bottom line. I loved you from the moment I saw you in Dallas."

Her heart felt as if it would burst. Tears drizzled from her eyes.

"Marry me, Gina." His voice cracked with raw, undisguised emotion.

She couldn't say no. Wouldn't have if she could have, because the truth of the matter was that she'd waited for this moment, longed for it, even when her pride had been battered, her bravado masking her pain. "Of course I'll marry you," she whispered, and felt his lips claim hers again. This solitary man loved her and she believed him. His lips molded over hers tenderly, with the promise of tomorrow and when he lifted his head, their future shone in his eyes. "I love you, too."

"I know."

A smile began to stretch from one side of his face to the other.

She actually giggled. This was serious. They were going to get married. She was going to be Mrs. Trent Remmington. She laughed out loud and Trent's deep chuckle echoed around the room. He held her tight and she clung to him. Oh, God, how could she have ever doubted him?

"Glad you're back with us." Garrett Kincaid was suddenly at her bedside, with Blake. "You gave us all quite a scare."

"Especially Trent," Blake added, touching her hand. "Now—" he looked at Garrett "—I think we should let the nurses' station know that the patient has awakened and then these two—" he hitched his chin toward Trent and Gina "—can have a few minutes alone before the real doctor comes along."

"So now you're a fake," Trent said, smiling. "I suspected it all along."

"I'm just not the M.D. in charge."

He and Garrett walked to the door, but Garrett turned and said, "You get better right quick, Gina. You still have another one of my grandsons to find."

"Will do," she promised.

"After you marry me," Trent insisted, and then, next to the hospital bed, he knelt and took her hand in his. "I came back to Whitehorn with this," he said, reaching into his pocket and extracting a ring—a gold band with a single diamond that winked brightly under the harsh hospital lights. "And then I thought that I might not ever be able to give it to you. Maybe I should do this the right way." He lifted her hand and, disregarding the IV drip, slipped the ring onto her finger. "Gina Henderson, will you marry me?"

Tears flooded her eyes. "I don't know what to say. I, um, I think you have me at a disadvantage here." She motioned to the IV stand. "No tellin' what they've slipped into my bloodstream." He lifted that damnably sexy dark eyebrow and waited. "Didn't I already say I would?"

"I'd like to hear it again."

"Okay, Remmington. It's a date. I'd love to marry you," she said saucily.

Again he laughed. "Then we'll make it as soon as possible. Just so you don't change your mind."

"Wouldn't dream of it. As soon as I get out of here."

"You're on, lady." He leaned over and kissed her lips. Gina's heart melted. God how she loved him.

Footsteps thundered in the hallway. In a second her brother Jack burst through the door. "Gina? My God, I'm sorry I couldn't get here any faster." He strode to her bedside and ignored Trent. "Are you all right?"

"Just fine," she said, seeing the worry in his eyes. "And there's something else you should know—you're going to be an uncle."

"Wait a minute—A *what?*"

"And I want you to give me away."

"Hey, slow down a minute. Are you delirious?"

"Not a chance, big brother. This handsome man here is Trent Remmington. He's about to become your brother-in-law."

Two weeks later Gina stood at the top of the stairs of the Kincaid house. With the help of the local wedding planner, Meg Reilly, she'd managed to put together a quick wedding. All of Trent's half brothers had shown up.

"You look beautiful," her mother said, kissing

Gina's cheek as Meg adjusted her veil. All three women's faces were visible in the small cracked mirror over Gina's bureau.

"And you look pretty good for a grandmother."

Her mother pulled a face. "I'm much too young to be a grandmother," she said, then laughed. "But I'm delighted, nonetheless. Now, I think I'd better take a seat downstairs," she said. "I just wish you were going to live in L.A."

"I told you that's impossible. Trent and I agreed to stay here in Whitehorn. And besides, I still have another one of Larry's sons to find, a baby."

"Work, work, work. You'll have a baby of your own to take care of."

"Yes, and he'll probably be born before I find that last one," Gina teased, and thought Meg seemed uncomfortable with the conversation.

"I think it's about time," Meg said with a wistful smile. "Your mother's right. You look fabulous."

"Thanks." Gina glanced out the window to the sprawling acres above which the vast Montana sky stretched. Cattle were grazing and a lone white stallion raced along the fenceline, his head lifted high and proud. She felt as if she belonged here in Montana, on the ranch. With Trent.

The first chords of the piano announced her entrance, so she hurried to the top of the stairs where Jack, as nervous as if he were the bridegroom, waited. "You sure about this?" he asked.

"More sure of it than anything in my life." She descended the stairs, following a trail of rose petals Mitch Fielding's twins had spread.

Jack's arm was steady and as they walked through the French doors to the backyard, Gina smiled brightly. Her family and Trent's family, along with a few of the good citizens of Whitehorn, Montana, had gathered around a hastily built arbor where Trent, dressed in a black tuxedo, was waiting for her. Joy pulsing through her veins, she released Jack's arm and walked forward to join the man who was going to be her husband.

He didn't wait for the reverend's approval, but lifted her veil before the ceremony and placed a kiss upon her lips. "For luck," he whispered, and her heart squeezed.

"Believe it or not, I don't need any," she confided as if no one else could hear. "Today I just happen to be the luckiest woman in the world."

Epilogue

"Well, Laura, that's that. Trent and Gina are married," Garrett said as he stood on the outside of the crowd. Colored lights had been strung on the porch and a band was playing country music. The bride and groom were dancing together, holding each other tight, acting as if no one else in the universe existed, though there were others on the makeshift dance floor with them.

"I didn't expect that, but it's a good thing, and that little great-grandbaby of ours deserves this." He chuckled and refused to think about the fact that Jordan Baxter seemed determined to make trouble for them.

He glanced at the rest of Larry's sons and wondered what would become of them. Cade Redstone had been particularly quiet this evening. He'd joined in the celebration, but hadn't said much, and as Garrett spotted him now, he was seated by himself, his thoughts turned inward.

Garrett sighed. "We can only hope that all of the boys end up as happy as Trent is tonight. I think he might even try to make amends with Blake, you know. Gives his brother the credit for saving the baby's life."

Garrett looked up to the stars. "I sure do miss you, Laura," he admitted, and felt the old familiar tug on his heart, "but then, I know you're watching down on us here." His eyes sparkled. "I wouldn't put it past you to have set this whole scene up yourself. You were always the matchmaker."

Again he looked at the bride and groom. "Well, darlin', this time you couldn't have done better if you'd tried."

* * * * *

Silhouette®

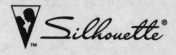

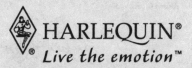

HARLEQUIN®
INTRIGUE®

BREATHTAKING ROMANTIC SUSPENSE

Shared dangers and passions lead to electrifying
romance and heart-stopping suspense!

Every month, you'll meet six new heroes
who are guaranteed to make your spine tingle
and your pulse pound. With them you'll enter
into the exciting world of Harlequin Intrigue—
where your life is on the line
and so is your heart!

THAT'S INTRIGUE—
ROMANTIC SUSPENSE
AT ITS BEST!

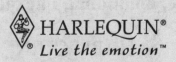

HARLEQUIN®
Live the emotion™

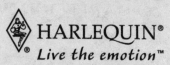